"Why are you here, Remi?" Her voice trembled and she got angry with herself for becoming a blubbering idiot at the mere sight of her former sweetheart.

"That should be obvious. I came here to see you, Camille."

"You wha… Why? I don't unders—"

He didn't wait for her to finish whatever it was she was going to say. He closed the distance between them and didn't hesitate to place his large, warm hands on either side of her neck, using the pads of his thumbs to gently stroke her cheeks as if coaxing her to comply with his unspoken demand.

Shock, lust, confusion and longing snaked its way to every crevice of Camille's body. The overwhelming sensations made her dizzy. She was so busy trying to figure out what was going on that she had not even realized that it was already happening. His lips had found hers and he indulged in helping her remember times past.

When she started to respond with soft moans, his fingers curled tightly into the hair at the nape of her neck. Remi pulled back, but only a fraction, leaving their lips achingly close.

Dear Reader,

As a transplant from a large city to a small town, I found it interesting how impassioned and proud people can be about the place in which they live, especially when everyone knows everyone.

This story is about how the dynamics of a small town can influence the way betrayal and devotion are depicted.

Remington Krane is a man who represents what it means to be successful, loyal and spirited about everything he sets out to do and has done in his hometown. His ex-love, Camille Ryan, spent ten years gaining her success elsewhere, leaving her town behind.

Their separation won't stop the passion that ignites when Remington steals one kiss, reminding Camille that she is and will always be his, and shows their town how years of beliefs can change when there is unconditional love and passion.

Enjoy!

Carla Buchanan

RETURN *To* PASSION

Carla Buchanan

HARLEQUIN® KIMANI™ ROMANCE

Recycling programs
for this product may
not exist in your area.

ISBN-13: 978-0-373-86460-7

Return to Passion

HARLEQUIN®
www.Harlequin.com

Printed in U.S.A.

Carla Buchanan was raised in California, but now lives in the Southern Belle world of Georgia. She likes to use the twists in her life to bring her readers fun, edgy and contemporary romances. She has a small obsession with her craft, and you'd find her any day of the week writing or out and about trying to find inspiration for her next story. She is delighted when readers reach out to her and would love to hear from you. She can be contacted through social media or directly on the contact page on her website at carlabuchanan.com.

Books by Carla Buchanan

Harlequin Kimani Romance

Return to Passion

To my husband, Isaiah Buchanan,
who constantly teases me about my love for words but
never asks me to stop writing them. Thanks for all
you've done in helping me reach my goals. I love you!

Chapter 1

Camille Ryan swung her desk chair around, not wanting to look at the computer screen one moment longer. She'd been in a state of mini writer's block all day long. She was stuck on this one scene and she didn't know why since she knew exactly where she wanted the story to go. Why was she so off tonight? Something was niggling at her and she couldn't seem to focus on anything, especially not writing. She was having one of those feelings you get when you know something is wrong, you just don't know what that something is.

Camille had often had feelings that she knew were something more, maybe a keener women's intuition, but ignored them. Her father said that it was her intuition telling her something; she just had to figure out what it was. According to her father, her mother had been the same way. Camille wondered if it *was* the truth since she'd never had a chance to meet Elaine Ryan. Her mother had died during childbirth and it had been her and her father ever since. Well, it used to be, until Camille had moved to New York when she was eighteen years old. She and her dad weren't as close as they used to be. It was only natural, she figured. After all, she couldn't take care of him forever, though she probably would've stayed closer to home if she had not gotten the internship in New York or hadn't been trying to do the right thing by the people she loved the most... Well, she wouldn't think about *that* situation right now. It was buried long ago so there was no need to bring old feelings of guilt bubbling to the surface.

An hour after trying and failing to type something on the page, Camille quit working. It was no use. She couldn't write erotic romance while wayward thoughts invaded her mind. She decided to call her father to check on him and make sure everything was okay. She'd talked to him the day before and knew he had a doctor's appointment today. The only conclusion Camille kept coming to was that he'd gotten bad news. She was so in tune with the man that she could sense the bad news deep down in her gut. That *had* to be what was bothering her. Her father had told her that it was just a routine checkup, but that didn't mean anything. On a few of those occasions she'd had to find out from other family that her father had gone to the hospital. It had hurt Camille that she had not been there for her father. It had hurt her even more that he hadn't told her, making her feel like she wasn't a good daughter. But she knew it was her father and his irrational logic. He had this crazy idea that not telling her things protected her. In fact, it only worried her.

The worrying intensified and her chest tightened when she tried calling him now. The phone just rang and rang. On the fourth call, the line connected to his voice mail immediately. Camille wasn't sure what was going on, but she knew something was wrong so she dialed her cousin. The news she got had her up and off her bed in a flash, throwing clothing haphazardly into suitcases and trying to make reservations at the same time.

Tired was a mild word to describe the way her body felt when Camille walked through Hartsfield-Jackson Atlanta International Airport in search of the baggage-claim area. She was cursing under her breath because each and every time she flew back here, the airport got more and more confusing.

It had been some years since she'd been to her hometown and even then it had been a quick visit where she had to sign some papers and then leave for an engagement or meeting she couldn't miss. And all the other visits before had been similar. Camille did not like running into people when she went home. Nor did she like hiding from everyone. They had an idea in their heads about who she was and she never wanted them to find out she wasn't the innocent little girl she'd been when she was simply "daddy's girl" in her hometown of Fairdell, Georgia, *and* she wasn't the evil girl who'd left so abruptly for her own selfish reasons.

Her reasons for leaving Fairdell hadn't been selfish;

rather they'd been *selfless*. Her reasons were one thing, but her secret was the kind that people in her tiny Bible-belt town wouldn't appreciate. So Camille had chosen to stay away. She didn't need their judgment. Plus, she didn't need to run into the one person who could possibly break her down and make her stay around. He'd see right through her. He'd make her want to tell him the truth—admit why she couldn't stay in Fairdell with him when they'd made plans—and he wouldn't approve of her reasons, especially since she'd left without talking to him first.

No, she couldn't see Remington Krane.

Remington rose from the ergonomic swivel chair and rubbed his hand down the stubble on his caramel-colored face. He knew he wouldn't shave, though. He kept this slight bit of facial hair because of her. She'd always said he looked good with the bit he had as a teen and even though they weren't together any longer and it had been years since he'd seen her, he still liked knowing that she'd appreciate the beard if she saw it.

She'd never come back to see it, though.

And why did he care what she thought? He shouldn't. He didn't. The girl—who was undoubtedly a woman now—was not what should be on his mind right now. She'd been out of his life for ten years. She'd chosen to leave him even when they'd made plans and had talked about the dreams they'd share and the future they'd have. He'd waited two years for her to graduate from high school so they could make their plans a reality, only to have her abandon him.

He'd been in love. They'd both been in love as two teenagers could be.

He'd been in college and had already started working for his grandfather as he waited for her. The plans were set. She would teach at the local high school. He'd work for his grandfather's company and one day he'd take over. Eventually he'd take his career even further by getting elected to political office: his influence, conservative nature and religious beliefs would be sure to help him along. They'd be the ideal couple everyone admired. That was the plan, but she'd changed it on her own and never bothered to let him know. That was what confused him most of all. It was so abrupt and unlike Cam—

Stop doing this to yourself, Remi.

Remington knew she was in his head because of the news he'd heard earlier about her father. Reese Ryan was too humble and hardworking for his own good. He never said no to anyone and took care of others before he took care of himself. He'd always been that way.

Remi once thought the landscaper was indestructible, the type who could work from sunup to sundown in ninety-degree weather. However, having an eighty-percent blockage in the heart valves would slow any man down and Remi only hoped the man would heed the doctor's advice and take care of himself.

But he doubted Mr. Ryan would be able to do so on his own for a while, which meant Camille would soon be in town. She'd come home a few times over the years but she'd never taken the time to visit anyone. She had not even visited her best friend often, not that he minded too much since her best friend was a guy.

Camille Ryan may have been twenty-eight and all grown-up now, but he'd always known her to be daddy's little girl. She loved her father endlessly and she wouldn't just breeze through town for something so serious. She'd stay around for a while, and Remington planned to use that time to his advantage. He'd get answers as to why she'd left. He needed to know why she'd chosen New York over him when she'd never mentioned a desire to live there. If she'd just told him, he would've supported her and they could've figured something out. They could have—

He stopped his racing thoughts. First things first. He had to get some work done if was going to acquire this plot of land Krane Gourmet Snack Foods needed to expand and build their frozen foods division, or he'd have to deal with his ever-unsatisfied grandfather.

It was ironic to think of Camille and then think of his grandfather. Camille had tried her best to be nice to the man, but Frederick Krane was stubborn and set in his ways. Frederick had a vision of Remington's future and it didn't include Camille Ryan.

From the moment Remington had started dating, his grandfather had encouraged him to be more than just friends with the daughter of a local judge whose family had been a part of his life since Remington could remember.

The daughter, Sonya Brandt, had never been Remi's type from the beginning. She was spoiled and selfish and entitled. There wasn't anything down-to-earth about her. She had annoyed Remington with the way she'd acted as if they were a couple just because of their families' expectations. But to please his grandfather, he'd let it go on for the most part, not really encouraging the girl or discouraging her. That was until a beautiful brown-skinned beauty had caught his eye and changed his world.

That memory made his thoughts return to her.

Camille Ryan.

The name still stirred something within him. They'd been mere teenagers when they were together but he knew from the first moment he'd laid eyes on her, with her glowing bronze skin, long thick hair and petite frame, that he'd be hooked for life. And he was. Despite time and distance, he still felt something for her and thought of her often over the years.

What would she do when she got to town? Would she seek him out? He doubted it. The girl he knew was not the type to renege on a decision so she'd probably stick by whatever reason had kept her away all these years. But she *had* reneged on a decision, hadn't she? He couldn't deny that, but his Camille was smart and he was sure if he heard her reason, he'd understand. The only conclusion Remington had been able to come to over the years was that Camille had changed her mind about him and their future and had been too afraid to tell him. He hoped that was the reason because he wasn't sure how he'd handle it being anything else.

Are you still in love with her?

He ignored the question.

When Remington had confronted Camille's father

all those years ago, he hadn't been any help either. The older man had told him nothing other than to respect her decision to change her mind. When he'd asked Mr. Ryan when she had changed her mind, he had told Remi that going to New York had always been her choice, but Remi would bet his life that wasn't true. He wasn't one to question his elders so he'd let it go. But Remington was sure Camille wouldn't just make plans with him and then suddenly change them without telling him something first.

Reese Ryan and Camille Ryan were the best of friends as well as father and daughter. The man would never have betrayed her trust if she'd asked him to keep the truth a secret.

Remi had forced himself to talk to Camille's best friend, Charleston Cobb, and while the man had not been very forthcoming, there were a couple details he *had* disclosed. Instead of returning to Fairdell to teach as she'd always planned, she'd chosen to stay in New York and teach at a private school of all things. As far as Remi knew, she still taught there. He'd also found out she was doing some sort of independent work. Teaching night classes or something, he guessed. That work was probably what had allowed her to pay off the mortgage on her father's house. Charleston had never told him what that additional job was and he had a feeling that the man had been secretive on purpose to keep him guessing or prove he knew more about Camille than Remi. Charleston had been so proud of his friend that he'd slipped and told Remi the name of the lavish apartment building in which Camille resided. It was a piece of information that would help him out in the future.

Remington could admit that there was a possibility he didn't know Camille at all—that he'd never really known her. However, that wasn't something he could accept.

He had to redirect his thoughts.

Focusing on work was what he would do now. He needed to get the company lawyer into his office to talk details on the land acquisition, which was an exercise in patience since the attorney in question happened to be Sonya. She insisted on flirting with him every time they were in each other's presence as if it were her right to do so. He'd told her he didn't mix business with pleasure but Sonya apparently didn't accept that explanation, believing she had a "special" place in Remi's life—his future. One-sided thinking on her part. He'd fire her, but she was a damn good lawyer even though she'd only been practicing for a few short years.

When Sonya sauntered into his office, Remington rolled his eyes. He wondered why he'd ever given her any attention, but admitted it was at a time when he had been really vulnerable. But that was all Sonya had needed. She'd used their one time together nearly ten years ago as a stepping-stone to what they could have in the future. Though he'd told her he wasn't interested in her, she insisted their union was best for them and their families, especially if he wanted to delve into the political arena as he'd always dreamed.

He agreed that her family had the influence to put him in office, but at what cost to his happiness? He didn't love Sonya; in fact, he could barely tolerate her on most occasions. However, though Krane Gourmet Snack Foods was the epitome of a company that got ahead by sticking to the values it began with and by helping the community, he'd still need an extra push to get him elected. The Brandts could be that push, but being with Sonya would be in direct conflict with what Krane Foods stood for. There'd be nothing moral in trying to fool the good people of Fairdell by pretending to be in love with Sonya. He cared for the town and the people too much to lie to them and trick them into voting for him.

Remington liked to think he didn't need such schemes to get him where he wanted, though he was sure his grandfather would disagree vehemently. He'd say Remington needed to think about the bigger picture and focus on happiness later. But there was a chance happiness had flown into town already and was walking around somewhere close. He doubted Frederick Krane would agree with that assessment of Camille's arrival, but Remi was an adult and no longer a child trying to get the approval of his family. He had a feeling his grandfather would one day realize that what he wanted for Remi wasn't necessarily what Remi needed.

Why he thought it would somehow all work out in the end was beyond him, but Remington was an optimist.

Chapter 2

Camille had finally negotiated the busy airport, found her luggage and gotten a rental car. She'd driven the hour to her hometown, going straight to the hospital and not bothering to stop by home. She'd been told her father had collapsed, flatlined and had to be revived. He'd been through a lengthy surgery to clear a blockage in his arteries overnight and couldn't do much on his own right now.

The scene before her was so much worse and Camille now realized why her father had tried to keep her away on his previous trips to the hospital. Seeing him so helpless and defeated was something her mind couldn't process fully. She only knew him as the man who rarely sat still because he loved being out and around his community and his landscaping business allowed him to do that.

Would he be able to continue at the pace he'd been going?

The easy answer to that was no.

And Camille would be around to make sure he took care of himself.

She only hoped he would allow her to take care of him.

Her cousin Augusta had told her over the phone that her father had been working long hours. The weather was too hot for even the healthiest, youngest person, let alone an almost fifty-year-old who'd suffered various ailments off and on over the years. Camille didn't know why her father chose to push himself so hard. She'd offered to make his life easier by taking care of some of the bills, but he wouldn't hear of such a thing. He'd told her that he was the one who was supposed to look after her, no matter her age, and she'd allowed him to do that for the most part. He didn't know about her career and the comfortable life she'd been able to have since she'd started writing so he probably thought she was overextending herself on what he thought was a teacher's salary. She'd had to go behind his back and pay off the mortgage on her childhood home, explaining away the money by saying she'd been doing some extra work outside the school. It had hurt her heart to lie to him, being that she was so proud of her writing career, but that's the way it had to be for his sake.

Camille had left town for Reese Ryan just as much as she had for Remi. She had not wanted them to deal with the fallout once people in town found out about the erotic books she wrote. She had not wanted to ruin her father's reputation or derail Remi's future. Her father's landscaping business was his life, just as Krane Foods and political aspirations were Remington's. Her career as a writer of erotica hadn't fit into normal, honorable, politically correct lifestyles ten years ago and it certainly did not now with all the success she'd acquired thus far.

But who knew... Maybe Remington was no longer the person she'd known—smart and loyal, with giant goals and a staunch moral compass. Maybe he was more like his grandfather, Frederick Krane. Maybe he'd changed and had let ambition and the need to be on top make him lax in his beliefs.

However, Camille couldn't believe that at all.

Besides, now wasn't the time to focus on Remington. Shaking away her thoughts, she gave all of her attention to her sick father and his recovery.

"Camille?"

She heard her name being called and turned to see her father attempting to sit up. She scrambled from her chair to fluff his pillows but he shooed her away with a scratchy, mumbled gripe. He muttered something about people not listening to him when he said not to call, but she ignored him and continued to help.

Camille stood next to her father's bed and took his hand in hers. He looked a little ashen but okay otherwise now that he was sitting up. He was a tough man so she expected nothing less.

"How are you feelin', Daddy?"

"Like I've been walking through the desert for days

with no water, but I'll be fine, Bug," her father said using the nickname he'd given her as a girl. He'd not called her that in a long time and she smiled at the nostalgic feeling that warmed her upon hearing it.

"I'm so sorry, Daddy. I should've—"

"You should've what? There was nothing you could do. You think you being here would've stopped my heart from giving out? No, it wouldn't have," he said sharply and coughed. Camille gave him water and he drank greedily. She didn't want him getting upset and she knew talk of what she should've or could've done would do just that.

"Daddy... I—"

"No. Listen to me." The struggle it took him to talk was making Camille uncomfortable. She wanted to urge him to rest but she doubted he'd listen. "I did this to myself. I admit I haven't been taking care of myself like I should. I could eat better and rest more. From now on I'll do that. You don't have to uproot your life for your old man, Bug." Once those words left his lips, he started to cough again. A nurse finally came in and presented him with the Popsicle she said she'd promised him earlier. Camille laughed because it was clear that the woman was flirting with her father and he was flirting back.

After her father ate a little and had fallen asleep again, Camille went out to call her agent. She updated Anna Vinson on her father's condition and gave her a rough estimate of when she expected to return. Anna wished her well and encouraged her to take a meeting or two while she was there, though Camille wasn't sure if she'd be able to do so without hiring someone to help with her father. She often took meetings as a "representative" of Reese Elaine, her pen name, so no one would know she was the person behind the books. It was her way of keeping everyone protected and safe from her secret career.

Twenty minutes after her call, Camille sat in the cafeteria waiting for the home health nurse to meet her. Camille's cousin Augusta had arranged the meeting because the woman was a friend of hers. Camille was sure this would be a formality since her cousin didn't deal with unsavory, unreliable or un-Christian-like individuals. It was how most people in this town were, which was what had kept Camille at a distance over the years. A small Southern town where the Bible was law and any deviation was blasphemous was not somewhere she could see herself living out her dream.

A short talk with the nurse was all she needed to feel reassured about her suitability. Now she had the rest of her day ahead of her. She decided to call Augusta, tell her she'd hired the nurse and go get a nap in before she returned to the hospital that evening.

As Camille walked into the lobby, she heard the women at the desk talking. They weren't trying to whisper and Camille was sure she heard her name followed by a couple insults. When she turned, one of the women she recognized as an ex-classmate gave her a sneer. Shrugging it off, Camille put the barbs behind her, knowing they were something she'd have to deal with because of her history with Remington Krane.

That was a name she tried not to think about, but she

had to admit it was him every other thought had gone to since she'd found out about her father. She wondered if she'd see him while she was in town, if he even wanted to see her. She wouldn't blame him if he didn't. She'd left him all those years ago and had not looked back. She'd done what she thought was best for herself *and* Remi, as well as her family and the town in general.

Remington knew Camille was in town. He knew because he'd heard the gossips talking about her when he'd gone to visit Reese Ryan. They'd been hard on her, which in turn had been hard for him to listen to despite his own need for answers about her departure.

The good news was that Reese Ryan was doing fine and would make a full recovery in a couple weeks. That was all that mattered to Remington because he was sure it was what mattered to Camille.

Now it was time to find the man's daughter. But first he had to see his grandfather, who'd summoned him to his large estate.

"Have you moved on that property?" That was the first thing that passed Frederick Krane's lips when Remi walked through the doors of the old man's sitting room. Remington wanted to curse the man for being so insensitive, but you couldn't teach an old dog new tricks, and his grandfather was the oldest dog of them all. He was set in his ways and didn't much like Remi's way of doing things. He said Remi wasn't cutthroat enough and that would be his downfall. But the man had not hesitated to hand over the business to Remi when he became ill, knowing that despite his constant gripes,

Remi had the right skills to run Krane Gourmet Snack Foods. In addition to that, Remi knew the old man loved him dearly, despite his disapproval.

"Aren't you going to ask me how Reese Ryan is doing? He *is* a respected business owner in this town, Granddad." Remington walked over to the chair facing his grandfather and sat down. "He is also a member of your church, a deacon and assistant superintendent of Sunday school. He's a perfect representative of what Fairdell is about, plus he's Camille's father and—"

"It always comes back to *her*, doesn't it? Boy, didn't you get enough of her abuse when she left you here with your tail between your legs? You know that was the best thing that happened to you, right? The Kranes did not need to have any familial associations with the likes of the Ryans. They aren't worthy of our time. God forgive me saying it but the Ryan girl is probably more suited for a good roll in the hay, maybe, but never more than that. You know where your future lies and it's not with Camille Ryan." He wiped his nose with a tissue but didn't skip a beat. "And speaking of church, it's about time for Krane to make its back-to-school donation. The mothers of the church have agreed to help give out supplies. I've volunteered you to help Sonya with making sure it gets done. Now Sonya, that is a hot little number *and* her family has the right connections. She's the one you need in your life and for your future. Judge Brandt is a moral, God-fearing man who's taught his daughter and son what it means to be successful. Long ago, her father and yours said you'd be together and I plan to honor your dad's dying wish."

Remington had heard this argument time and time again. He knew his grandfather didn't like Camille because he thought her father's job was beneath them. However, though Remi did not agree, he didn't argue. His grandfather would surely have another heart attack if he got him too riled up. But one thing he would not let his grandfather do was tarnish his father's memory.

"Granddad, you know that was not my father's dying wish."

"You may be right about that, but it's mine. And you don't have to wait 'til I'm dead to make that happen. They say, give them their flowers while they live and Sonya is one stunningly gorgeous flower. But about that land—" His statement was cut off by a sudden coughing fit.

The home nurse ran into the room and Remington took that as his opportunity to leave. This had happened many times during his visits so he felt no guilt in leaving. The old man would hardly recognize that he was gone now that his nurse's ample cleavage was in his face.

Chapter 3

Speaking with Charleston "Charlie" Cobb was nothing new. Camille spoke to him often. He was not only her lawyer, he was her best friend, and she loved him. She had no idea where she'd be without having him to complain to or get advice from. He was one of the main reasons she'd quit her teaching job and had gone after her dream. He was behind her all the way and had even paid her rent for a couple months when she didn't renew her teaching contract so she could focus on writing full-time.

He had accompanied her when she visited her father the second time that day, and had returned home with her. Charlie had then left to run an errand and she'd fallen asleep after a shower, only to be woken up now by a pounding on the door. She had no idea who it was until she remembered that Charlie was supposed to come by after he was done with his errand. Waking up in her old living room had thrown her off and she had no idea he'd return so soon.

He came in with his commanding presence, protective attitude and a six-pack of beer, fussing at her for not asking who was at the door. He pushed past her like he owned the place, heading straight to the kitchen. "Thanks for letting me read those pages," he said and she looked at him as he returned with a bottle of water. "I think they worked."

"Eww…you're using my stories as a guidebook? That's nasty, Charlie."

Charlie plopped down on the couch and put his feet on the ottoman. "Hey, you shouldn't be so good. And it's not the first time…and it won't be the last."

"Eww… Do I know this person?"

"Doubtful, but she kinda puts me in mind of my career rival here in town—your *best friend*."

Best friend? She knew what that meant. He meant her one and only *enemy*, Sonya Brandt. Last Camille had heard she was the lawyer for Krane Foods, which was the most Camille had allowed Charlie to tell her about Fairdell when they talked. He'd informed her that Sonya had been hired with the blessing of Frederick Krane, and their two families had been closer than ever since she'd been working there. That was perfect since Sonya always wanted and felt she was entitled to have Remington anyway. Now she was probably having him anytime she wanted.

Camille wasn't sure why that thought didn't sit well

with her. She didn't even want to begin to guess why her mind had gone there.

Camille hated having negative thoughts about anyone, but Sonya was a special case. Camille had often wondered how the woman ever got through law school because during high school she'd never done any schoolwork. It was possible that she'd had others do it for her and that trend probably continued through college. Camille wouldn't put anything past her. Sonya Brandt was spoiled and stuck up and thought she was God's gift to men because her father was white and her mother was black. She thought that made her exotic and irresistible.

"Hey, babe, I'm going to go get a beer. I thought I could wait for the food, but I can't," Charlie declared once the conversation hit a lull. She'd missed him and often felt guilty that he had to keep her secret. He was her best friend and was often the one answering the questions people asked about her because he lived in Fairdell. He was more like an overprotective big brother than a best friend most times.

The brief silence gave way to thoughts of Remi.

She hadn't been able to get away from those ever since she'd arrived in town. She couldn't help thinking about him even when she didn't want to. But now was not the time. She had other things to worry about, like her father and his return home. She had to make sure the house was clean and there was food in the fridge. She had to—

"I think I hear a car in the driveway," Charlie hollered from the kitchen. "It's probably the pizza guy. I left some money on the coffee table."

She rolled her eyes. Sometimes Charlie forgot about what she now did for a living. She could afford a lot more than a pizza, though she tried to live modestly. She bought the things she desired and she lived the lifestyle she wanted—within limits. Her only splurge was paying off her father's mortgage. It was the least she could do for the man who'd raised her by himself.

She fished the bills off the table, not having time to go get her purse from the room upstairs. She flung the door open and giggled—the wine she'd been sipping was kicking in. She probably shouldn't have drunk it on an empty stomach but she'd needed the stress reliever after her flight and visit to the hospital.

She might just guzzle the whole bottle on the next go 'round…or maybe not, because she was hallucinating. How else could she explain seeing Remington Krane standing at the door of her home?

"Long time."

Camille was speechless. She'd heard him speak but was still so much in shock that nothing came out except for an embarrassing hiccup courtesy of the wine. And then she took him in. His height, strong facial features, the shaved head and slight beard, the smoothness of his caramel skin, and the very manly scent emanating from his direction made her drift closer to him.

The man was sexy and the sight of him made her libido spring to life.

Camille's mouth opened and closed until finally she took a step back and said, "Why are you here, Remi?" Her voice trembled and she got angry with herself for becoming a blubbering idiot at the mere sight of her former sweetheart.

"That should be obvious. I came here to see you, Camille."

"You wha… Why? I don't unders—"

He didn't wait for her to finish whatever it was she was going to say. He closed the distance between them and didn't hesitate to place his large, warm hands on either side of her neck, using the pads of his thumbs to gently stroke her cheeks as if coaxing her to comply with his unspoken demand.

Shock, lust, confusion and longing snaked into every crevice of Camille's body. The overwhelming sensations made her dizzy. She was so busy trying to figure out what was going on that she had not even realized that it was already happening. His lips had found hers and he indulged in helping her remember times past.

When she started to respond with soft moans, his fingers curled tightly into the hair at the nape of her neck. Remi pulled back, but only a fraction, leaving their lips achingly close.

"Hey, babe, did the pizza get here?" Charlie said as he walked back into the room, obviously not realizing they had a visitor. "I had a hell of a time trying to find the bottle opener. You know you could've just left it on the counter."

Camille couldn't believe that she'd forgotten Charlie was in the house. She jerked back and when she nearly lost her footing, both men came to her aid before she ended up with her body parts intermingled with the wood of a nearby table.

A large, strong hand landed under each elbow. She was practically lifted from the floor when they righted her. Camille yelped a little and then stepped away from the men. They glared at one another before Charlie spoke first.

"I knew it wouldn't be long before you showed up." Charlie took a protective stance next to Camille, folding his arms over his bulky chest. Giving a welcoming look to Remi wasn't an option for Charlie. He didn't really care for Remi's more conservative, good-guy nature. He felt a man who was so loyal and "perfect" had something to hide, though Camille did not agree. Remington Krane was exactly who everyone believed him to be. He was *that* nice.

She had not even considered that Remi would seek her out. He had not done so in all these years and there was no doubt he had the means and time to do it. She figured he'd gotten over her pretty quickly and had moved on without much thought to what had happened. But, if that kiss and the look on his face was any indication, she was completely wrong. Not that she'd had much time to think clearly in the past few moments. Her brain was still trying to catch up to Remington Krane actually being here and on top of that, acting as if no time had passed between them. His behavior suggested that he was no longer angry with her for the way she left, but now Camille was left to decipher what it all meant. However, her traitorous body was telling her it didn't care about any of that.

Reeling in her libido, Camille stood tall and mimicked Charlie's stance. "Why are you here, Remi?" she asked again. She desperately wanted to have his lips on hers again, but that wasn't what she needed. She needed him to leave. She needed him to stay far away from her. He'd only reawaken feelings she'd kept hidden. She'd left for his sake—for their sake. Her leaving was supposed to be her liberating act—one that left them both free to realize their dreams.

"I'm here for you, of course."

Had Camille been expecting that response? No. Should she have expected nothing other than the confident man she knew he'd become? Probably.

"We don't know each other anymore, Remi. That was ten years ago and we were stupid teenagers. Stupid teenagers who made stupid promises they could never have kept. I left, Remi. Obviously you haven't heard. So, you should probably just…go."

Tears were forming and threatening to spill by the time she got out the last word. She didn't think saying the words would hurt *her* so much. She wanted to turn away so she could experience the full range of her emotions, but she needed to know if she'd hit her mark. Pushing back the tears, Camille squared her shoulders and waited.

"*Know you?* Well, that is a joke, isn't it? Of course I don't know you, Camille. I don't know the person who lied and said she would stand by me. I don't know the person who left without so much as a call or a note. You have some nerve, you know that? I should be angry with you. I should never want to speak to you again and here I am trying to—"

"Leave," Camille said in a low voice. Charlie was her

best friend and Remi was nothing more than an ex—
an ex whom she still needed to protect despite her true
feelings. "Leave, Remington! Get out now," Camille
said and balled her fists at her sides. She then looked
at Charlie and he nodded his support, knowing why she
had to do this to Remi.

Remi noticed their eye contact, and he glanced from
one to the other. "You two together now? Is that what
this is about? You finally get her into bed, Charlie?"

Slap.

Camille could not believe she'd just done that and
stepped back shaking her hand while Remington held
the side of his face in astonishment. Although she had
to admit it had worked out perfectly. She'd provoked
him to anger and surely he'd leave now and forget about
her. It was why this whole act was necessary.

"I deserve that," Remi admitted. "I shouldn't have
said that and I'm sorry."

"I said leave, Remington, especially if this is all you
came here for." He really needed to remove himself
from the premises because she could almost feel herself slowly giving in. "Maybe…maybe we can talk…"

Had those words fallen from her lips? She'd meant
to think them, not say them aloud. Thankfully Remington said, "Forget it," and turned to walk toward the
door. "And just so you know… I forgave you a long time
ago," he said not looking back at her and then walking
out the door without another word.

Was this what gum on the bottom of someone's shoe
felt like? Probably pretty close to it. She'd known this
encounter would happen, but she didn't think it would

be this soon and she hadn't expected him to do *that* when he first saw her.

Camille didn't know what had driven Remington Krane to go through the trouble of actually stopping by, but he'd left her with a simple, sweet, memorable kiss that had so much power and meaning behind it. It would take a while to get over this, but she knew it was for the best.

What had come over him, he wasn't quite sure. Remington had gone over to that house to simply let Camille know that he was aware she was in town and that this time she wouldn't be hiding from him. He also wanted to tell her that he was sorry about her father and to offer his help in any way she needed.

But the visit had not gone that way.

She had opened the door before he'd had a chance to knock, catching him off guard. He'd planned to give himself a little pep talk before ringing the doorbell but seeing her had made him forget all that.

He'd looked down at her standing there with her mouth opening and closing like a cute little guppy and his little friend down below had started to throb as if asking him if they were both seeing the same thing. They were. Camille had stood there in a pair of sexy little lounge shorts and a tank top with no bra. He even guessed that she might have been panty-less since the shorts left little to the imagination.

His groin had done the moving for him as it took over and propelled him in her direction. He'd not intended to kiss her without even saying hello but other parts of him had other plans and he'd not been in control of his actions.

That was the story he was sticking to.

Then it had all gone to hell with her best friend being there. He knew the man thought of her as a little sister so he couldn't blame him for his protectiveness. However, when it got in his way, it was annoying.

It was easy to see she had not meant the words she'd yelled at him. It was even easier to *feel* how she'd responded to his touch. It had been unmistakable. The girl was a woman now and the woman had wanted him.

Remi drove through the streets of town trying to calm himself. He was angry with himself for not sticking to his plan, he was angry with Camille for her reaction to his presence, and he was angry with Charlie for simply existing.

The anger had him driving aimlessly around town, but somehow he had ended up right back at her house. He didn't go in this time but instead stood outside the gate. He looked over the fence at the shed. He and Camille had spent many a day making out in that shed when they were supposed to be completing a task for her father's landscaping business.

He smiled as he remembered when he and Camille had first started dating. Mr. Ryan would not allow Remi to set foot in his home. His daughter was only fifteen and a sophomore and he was about to be eighteen and a senior. Mr. Ryan had forbid his daughter to date until she was sixteen but she'd begged him to let Remi come over, vouching for his good nature. Her father was a pushover when it came to Camille and couldn't say no.

After that, Remi became a regular fixture at the Ryan home since Remi's grandfather had made it clear that he did not approve of his grandson dating someone with such a "common" background.

Remi stood in front of Camille's childhood home for a while longer before leaving. He noticed the light in her old bedroom was on and briefly watched as her silhouette passed the window. Seconds later the room went dark, which was his signal to stop acting like a stalker.

"God, please watch over the man who raised the woman I love and restore him to full health," he prayed before getting in his car and returning to his home.

Chapter 4

Two days after her arrival in town, Camille's father was released to her care and that of that home health nurse. He was given a better prognosis than she'd anticipated, along with the all-clear to return to normal activities as long as he cut down on some of his more strenuous ones.

She'd taken him home to find the nurse already waiting. Camille had cooked a small meal and prepared an area for her father to rest and relax. He'd grumbled and groaned as she'd helped him to the house, but his whole demeanor had changed when he'd laid eyes on the woman who'd be caring for his needs for the next week.

Now as she stepped into the grocery store, Camille thought about her life in New York for the first time in days. She'd have to return to her apartment soon. She had a profession that was ruled by deadlines and she needed to get in touch with her agent to discuss them. The woman was a barracuda and a shark and any other ferocious animal all rolled into one. She could find a bookstore in the middle of Antarctica to sell Reese Elaine books in if she so chose. And she'd done just that if her lengthy phone message that morning was anything to go by. Anna had arranged for Camille to meet with a potential distributor who was also a fan. The woman had agreed to not take any pictures if she could simply meet Camille, the woman attached to the pseudonym Reese Elaine. Her publishing team had wanted to do business with this distributor but it was too costly. The meeting would guarantee a substantial discount for them and make it happen. Camille was just glad she'd packed for this possibility.

To the world—the literary world—Reese Elaine was the author of ten full-length erotic novels and several novellas. Camille had pursued her writing dream at the encouragement of her high school English teacher after Camille had mistakenly turned in a few chapters of her work instead of an essay. The teacher had pulled her aside and given her an application for an internship in New York and had told Camille she had a real future in writing. It was all the encouragement she needed and had been the catalyst that had led her to New York, where she ended up pursuing her degree. Her life had changed that day.

Now she was no longer a teacher of tenth grade English at a private school and hadn't been for some time. She'd come this far and had not had to reveal her identity to anyone and didn't see herself doing so anytime soon. And by "this far" she meant a hefty contract for three of her books and even bigger ones for her next seven. It was truly a blessing to be able to do something she loved; she only wished that she could share the good news with her family and friends, but she knew that wasn't possible. She'd be putting her father's business and reputation in jeopardy. His clients, church members and friends might not understand that his daughter wrote what conservative people considered pornography.

Reese Elaine was the main reason she'd had to give up Remi. Krane Foods was considered a family-oriented business and her books were nothing of the sort. She couldn't allow Remi to give up his future for her so she'd chosen for him.

Camille was energized not only by her agent's message but also by that news she'd gotten over the phone a few minutes ago. She'd woken up feeling a little off, but after that conversation, she'd felt like singing. Her father's doctor had said his tests had all come back normal and after his recovery he'd be in better health than he had been in years.

She hurried home from the grocery store to share the results with him, but his reaction to the good news was less than enthusiastic.

"'Bout time you got back."

"Well, good to see you, too, Mr. Grumpy Pants. What has you in a bad mood?" Camille put a bag of food down on the coffee table and sat on the couch she remembered her and Remi making out on. The thought brought a smile to her face, but she wiped it away just as fast as it appeared.

"Not in a bad mood, just hungry. And it didn't help that I had to smell that crap in the kitchen. I bet they're doing something illegal with the packaging to get folks to buy the stuff. Some sort of subliminal scent or something, I bet! Like I said…illegal," Reese Ryan ranted.

Camille had not noticed the smell before but when she did, she couldn't help the bright smile that took over her face.

She'd recognize that smell anywhere. It was her favorite snack from Krane Gourmet Snack Foods and she'd eaten it ever since she could remember. She even made sure to buy up all the stock they had in her local corner market when they got it in. It was odd because no other market in the area—or in the city, that she'd noticed—sold the snacks except for this one store by her house. She'd always thought it was strange but she'd been grateful to have that one comfort from home.

She went into the kitchen and pulled up short.

"Oh. My. God." Camille had no idea what had gotten into Remington Krane but she was in awe. It hadn't been long since their encounter, but she figured that she wouldn't hear from him again after her attempt to reject him. But hear from him she did, and in the sweetest way…literally.

There on the counter of the kitchen was a beautifully arranged basket containing at least twenty bags of her favorite snack. There was a bright yellow card attached to the front that said "Read Me" instead of her name.

She opened it and another small plastic card fell out.

A gift card to a big chain office store with a four-figure amount attached, no doubt for supplies for her supposed teaching job. She cursed under her breath and then read the three handwritten sentences.

We start over tomorrow night at 7 p.m. with dinner. I'll pick you up at home. Wear my favorite color…please.

Camille had no idea what she should do. She knew she wouldn't be able to meet with him for dinner but that didn't mean she didn't want to. She'd had a chance to sleep on it and realized that she really, really wanted to know what that kiss had been all about. She wanted to tell him all about her career. She wanted to tell him about her life and hear about his. She wanted…

Camille wanted *him*.

She wanted Remington Krane.

She wanted to experience the things she wrote in her books. She wanted to be seduced and touched and treated like the sensual woman she knew she could be. She no longer wanted to feel like a fraud to her fans because she was a virgin. She was a woman who was raised in *this* town and its values had been ingrained in her. Despite her career, she still believed in saving herself for the one man she wanted to spend the rest of her life with.

If her fans knew, they'd boycott her books and demand refunds. That was probably an exaggeration, but she didn't want anyone to find out that each and every book was written about a fantasy she'd had about the very man who was now requesting her presence for dinner.

* * *

By now, his gift to Camille would have arrived and hopefully she'd have seen it. He knew it would be a hit regardless of whether they were at odds with one another or not. It was her favorite snack and would always be if he had anything to do with it. And he *did* have something to do with it since he'd found out where she lived after a conversation with Charleston and had personally sent the snacks to the nearest grocery store. He'd even contacted the owner personally to see if Camille frequented the store and when he found out that a woman matching her description had been coming in, he'd paid the man to carry the snack and point it out to her the next time she came in. She had no idea that Remi had done that and he'd do it again if she ever moved to a new place.

His behavior bordered on stalker since he knew where she lived and where she bought her groceries thanks to a little investigating.

He was allowing his thoughts to stray, taking his mind off of the land deal he should've been thinking about. His grandfather had called every day wanting to hear some information but Remi had dodged the man as usual. The land deal was under way but he wanted to handle it without his grandfather's interference. He loved his grandfather, but in his old age he'd started to stray from some of the core values of the company. He'd been touched by the demons of power, ambition and success, and he'd begun to believe they made him better than others—better than good people like Reese Ryan and his lovely daughter.

Making sure the land acquisition went smoothly should've been the only thing on Remi's mind but it wasn't. A pair of shapely bronzed legs, attached to a petite little frame that he could see himself buried deep inside of, was all his mind kept going back to. The way her womanly body—more alluring now than before— had appeared to him the other night should've been a sin. The doe-eyed look on her face when she had opened that door was one that he wouldn't mind seeing while she writhed underneath him.

Had she had sexual experiences over the years? Of course she had. She was a beautiful woman and had the smarts to back up the looks, so she'd have no trouble attracting men.

It tormented Remi to think about another man with his hands on what he'd always considered his. No matter the time and the distance, he'd always thought of Camille Ryan as his girl, though she'd left him.

Remington was startled from his thoughts when his phone rang. He answered it since his secretary didn't come in on Saturday. Neither did he on most Saturdays, but he was trying to take his mind off Camille and the fact that she could be leaving soon.

"Remington Krane," he said when he didn't recognize the number that showed up on the caller ID. He had a feeling that it might be Camille and if she was calling, then he hoped it wasn't to turn him down. He switched on the speaker so he'd have his hands free.

"Oh…hi, Remi. I got your gift and I thought I should call you and thank you." She paused and he could tell she was nervous. "They are still my favorite snack…

I—I want to say that, while I wish I could join you for dinner, I can't. I have an engagement in the city and won't be back in time." She rushed through the words and it gave Remi the slightest bit of satisfaction that she was uncomfortable turning him down.

Maybe the kiss hadn't been a total mistake.

"No problem at all," Remi said stopping her from continuing to let him down. "May I ask what type of engagement? I thought your trip to town was unexpected."

He knew he was fishing and that she had every right to tell him to mind his own business, but he wasn't ready to get off the phone and he did have a genuine interest in where Camille would be. He expected her to avoid the subject but instead she said, "I have a friend flying to the West Coast and she has a layover in the city. I told her I'd meet her for an early dinner."

Camille hated lying. He knew that about her and she was definitely lying.

"Oh, really. Where do you plan to take her? Maybe I could make some suggestions." He tried not to sound disappointed over being lied to.

She hesitated for a moment and then told him that she was open to suggestions. She listened intently, but something inside him told him she wasn't taking any of it in. She thanked him again and promised to call and reschedule, but as he hung up he knew he wouldn't hold his breath.

Camille wasn't sure why she felt so bad about having to let down Remi, but she did. She'd felt so bad about lying to him that she'd wanted to tell him exactly what she was going into the city to do. If anyone would be proud of her, Remi would. He'd probably go out and buy all her books just to see if she based any of the characters on him. Then he'd find something in every one and insist he deserved some sort of royalty payment for being her inspiration. Jokingly, of course, but he'd definitely say it.

Camille blushed at the mere idea of Remi reading words she conjured from her thoughts. It was one thing for a stranger to read her books but it was another for someone close to read them. It would be like them seeing a different side of her—a side that may suggest she wasn't as innocent as people imagined her to be.

Wasn't that her dilemma? She was doing this thing that she was so proud of and she could only be proud of it in secret. She was afraid to reveal the truth because she didn't want to hurt her family. She certainly didn't want to bring any unwanted attention to her small hometown. Using this alias had protected everyone, although she could honestly say she sometimes wished she didn't have to hide her identity. She wished she could tell everyone, especially Remi. She wished she could tell everyone that she'd only left to protect Krane Foods and Remi's future, because ultimately, she could've dealt with the scrutiny if had been just her she had to think about.

Chapter 5

The next day went by quickly. Her father had made breakfast, despite the protests of the home health nurse, and they'd talked and caught up a little. He told her he would not be sitting in the house another whole day and that he'd politely told the nurse that day would be her last, despite the fact that she'd been 'easy on the eyes'. Camille had wanted to object but had it on good authority from his doctor that he'd be fine on his own if he followed the rules given at the time of his discharge.

Before she knew it, she was pulling up to the restaurant where she was to meet the distributor. The valet took her keys and parked her car.

"Cami—I mean, Reese Elaine... There should be a party expecting me," she said to the snobby host giving her the once-over. If he only knew who she was, he wouldn't treat her that way. But she didn't write for the fame and that was clear since she'd chosen to remain anonymous all these years.

She followed the wiry blond-headed fellow to a private lounge area. When she walked through the door, she was surprised to see several women there, all looking like Southern beauties with their big pageant hair and perfectly applied makeup. Setups like this made Camille go into author mode. These ladies would make great characters for a book. *Maybe they could all be in love with the same guy...*

"So good to finally meet you, Reese." The woman who'd stepped forward took Camille's hand in her own and held it for a moment and then let go. The gesture kept Camille's thoughts from straying too far and being called by her father's name made her wince a little. The few people who knew her as Reese Elaine also knew her as Camille Ryan so she never got to hear the pseudonym from their lips.

"Nice to meet you as well, Colette. You *and* your lovely daughters." Camille had put the pieces together to this little carbon-copy celebration. These girls all looked so much alike that it was obvious they were all sisters. Hell, if she didn't know they weren't quintuplets, she would've thought that at first glance.

"I've read each and every one of your books. It would be an honor if you'd sign this for me."

The woman turned and one of her daughters who stood silently behind her handed Colette an e-reader. The device, as well as a silver paint-pen, was put into her hands and she wrote the requested message on the back.

After that, the evening became a little lighter. They all got to know each other and Camille realized that looks could be deceiving because these girls were a riot. They drank and laughed and they even tried to fix Camille up with their older brother who was a real-estate developer in town. She said she'd think about it, though she had no intention of getting anywhere near that. There was no way she could take this kind of attention on a regular basis. They asked her every question in the book and had even questioned her sexuality when she said she didn't date very often. They joked and said she must be really free with her sexuality and Camille had to remember that the girls were basing her experience on what she wrote in her books. She assured them that each and every book was a product of her vivid imagination, which led to a discussion of potential ideas for future books.

After a brief private meeting with Colette they came to a tentative deal on distribution rights. Colette said she'd be having her team contact Reese's publisher soon to hash out the details and then she left. Camille wanted to leave as well but the sisters begged her to stay. She agreed and they shoved a drink into her hand and moved their little party into the private bar area of the restaurant, saying Camille needed to have fun like her characters.

Camille decided to enjoy this one night. She was still on edge days after that kiss from Remi. Maybe a little attention was just what she needed that evening.

"Okay, you can't keep turning down every man that approaches you, Reese," Beth, the youngest sister, slurred.

"I'm not turning them down. I let two of them buy me a drink."

"Come on, Reese, let me pick someone for you. I promise I have good taste." Beth didn't wait for Camille to respond. She hopped off her stool and worked her way through the semicrowded bar area. Camille figured the woman wouldn't be back since the alcohol would probably hinder her mission. However, about twenty minutes later she got a tap on her shoulder and standing there with Beth was the last person she expected to see an hour away from their hometown.

"What are you doing here, Remington?"

"I'm beginning to think that's your favorite question."

"You two know each other?" The younger woman squealed. "Damn, I'm good! I have to go tell my sisters. Have fun and don't do anything I wouldn't do."

Remi never took his eyes off Camille. He stood there silently as if he knew something he shouldn't. And when he spoke, she nearly had a heart attack because she knew she had some explaining to do.

"I talked to Charlie. He wouldn't tell me much, but he did lead me to you, Ms. Reese Elaine. You didn't have to keep it from me, Camille," Remi said as he reached for her hand.

Camille breathed in deeply. She knew the conversation that was coming would be a serious one and she was slightly disturbed that Charlie would reveal her secret.

It had taken some persuading and some begging but Charlie had ultimately given some information. The information hadn't been much, only a name. But one simple search online, as well as a few purchases from the online book retailer, had been enough. The author's bio, as scarce as it was, had let him know Camille Ryan and Reese Elaine were one and the same.

Remi's visit to Charlie had been strategic, but had ended up feeling like one of his sessions with his pastor. He'd told her friend about his love and need for Camille and his desire to be with her forever now that he'd laid eyes on her again. He'd admitted to Charlie that it was expected of him to wed Sonya at some point and he probably would've eventually allowed his grandfather to talk him into it. However, fate had stepped in to stop the mistake he might have been forced to make.

Remi hated that it had taken a downturn in Reese's health to get Camille back to town, but her arrival had come right at a time when Remi had been contemplating the next step in his future. He'd submitted his petition to run for mayor of Fairdell and it would be nice to have his personal life as well as his professional life in order. Knowing it would take more than just a heartfelt confession to win over the man, he'd appealed to Charlie's's emotional side. He'd told him about the snacks he'd sent to her grocer. He'd told Charlie about the yearly donations he'd sent to her school. He'd mentioned the gift he'd sent to her home and had been surprised that the man did not know about it yet.

That was when Charlie had started to look uncomfortable. "You're sort of a stalker, you know that, Rem? Not very becoming of the business tycoon and potential future mayor, don't you think?"

"How did you…?" Only a few people knew about Remi's plans to run for mayor. It had made Remi realize how smart Charlie truly was and made him thankful Camille had the man on her side even though their friendship sometimes rubbed Remi the wrong way. "You know what…never mind. You're avoiding what you know I came here for."

Charlie had moved through his living room toward the fireplace. Sitting on the mantel had been a picture of Charlie and Camille. He'd picked up the picture and stared at it for a moment before putting it down. "What *did* you come here for, Rem? You've said a lot, but it really means nothing to me. I want to protect my friend. Your feelings are of no concern to me."

Offended, Remi had said, "What the hell is that supposed to mean? I'm trying here, Charlie. I'm trying to make you see how I feel. I know I need your blessing to go forward with her, but I also know you know her secret—why she's distancing herself from me. You can help me. I want to bring her back here. I want her here with me. I want—"

"What about what she wants?"

"I'm positive we want the same thing."

"How? From one little kiss? A promise you made to each other as naive teenagers? I thought you were smarter than that. It takes a lot more—"

"Don't you think I know that? It's why I'm here! You know I hate this as much as you but we're going to have to get along for her because I'm not backing off, Charlie."

"Can I ask you something?"

This question had come out much calmer than any other statement he'd said all evening. Remi had felt calm, as well. Anger was not the way to go if he was going to get Charlie to tell him anything about Camille.

"Sure."

"What the hell took you so long?"

Remi had let those words process, then immediately started chuckling. "You know what? I really don't know. I thought I was giving her what she wanted."

"This is Camille we're talking about. She'd rather protect everyone else than do what she knows she truly wants."

He'd suspected a deeper meaning there. Remi hadn't been sure if Charlie realized he'd let that slip. "Who is she protecting, Charlie?" The pointed look Charlie had given him had made it obvious that Remi was the one Camille was protecting.

"I'm not going to give you more than I should, but I know she has some unresolved feelings for you. The truth will set her free in more ways than just getting closure with you."

A name and a place written on a piece of paper had been what Charlie had given him.

After that, Charlie had drunk the rest of his liquor and had disappeared into another room, effectively dismissing Remi. Remi had sat there for a moment and then rushed out of the house. He'd raced home to his laptop and when he'd typed in the name Reese Elaine, he'd been surprised to see the magnitude of results. The one with the biggest number? Reese Elaine, author of women's fiction. *Number one* seller of women's *erotic* fiction, he'd had to correct himself after his research.

Camille was this anonymous, world-famous author. She'd become famous without ever having to make a public appearance and the literary world speculated that she could be so much more if she'd come forward and reveal herself.

This was why she'd left. She'd left to pursue this dream. But Charlie had said she was protecting him, as well. He'd sighed, knowing there was more to the story.

That woman. Camille Ryan. That beautiful, smart, selfless woman had sacrificed the future they'd planned so they could both have their dreams. Remi wasn't an idiot. He knew where they lived and he knew how conservative the town was. On a Sunday, you'd be hard-pressed to find someone not attending church somewhere. Even Frederick Krane spent his Sundays in God's house, which was saying a lot.

Then there was his responsibility to the company his grandfather had created. Krane Gourmet Snack Foods had been voted the most morally responsible company in the state and was top ten in the nation. And he had been slated to take the helm as president and CEO when his grandfather felt he had earned the position.

On top of Krane, there were Remi's political aspirations. He'd always dreamed of coming back to Fairdell after college and one day being a leader in his community, so he could serve them and care for them as they had for him growing up.

Remi could understand why Camille would choose to flee. If she had told him she was going to leave so his future would be secure, he'd have stopped her. He'd have supported her dream, but he wouldn't have let her give up their relationship, as well. He would've compromised and found a different way to achieve his dreams.

He would've resented her for her hand in that, eventually. And he would've lost her anyway.

Now, as he stood in front of her, he could see how much she still wanted to protect him. It made him angry that they couldn't just be who they were and love each other without worrying what other people would think and say. He should be the one protecting Camille, not the other way around. And he'd do that. He'd stand by her and make her realize she had the support of her family and friends.

Remi led Camille to a table that he'd reserved inside the restaurant. They sat quietly for several moments, letting Camille get her thoughts together. It didn't take long for her to confirm everything he had already figured out. He found out she'd been encouraged by her English teacher to apply for an internship in New York that would get her a scholarship at the end and get her work in front of an editor. She said she hadn't been sure if she'd take it, but she'd known it was a sign—an opportunity. She knew she'd be blamed for leaving him. She'd be hated. But in the end they'd both be able to follow their dreams. She thought he'd get over it eventually and move on, but little did she know that had not happened.

And that was clearly evident when he couldn't stop staring at the slick gloss that made her lips peel sexily apart each time they moved. It was only for the briefest of seconds, but it drew Remi's eyes to her mouth as he listened to her proper tone that had lost most of its Southern inflection. The dress she was wearing was very figure-flattering, and he was unable to take his eyes off her cleavage, so tastefully displayed. The neckline jutted straight down between her breasts and the fabric skimming the insides of those perfect mounds had to be held there by some sort of magic. He'd never seen her in anything like this and he wasn't sure he liked it, at least not for anyone else but him.

At the end of her confession, he didn't know whether he wanted to hold her, hate her or have her.

Camille suddenly stopped what she was going to say next and looked directly at him—something she hadn't done during her ramble. "What? Why are you looking at me like that?"

"No reason. Please continue," he tried to say in a way that didn't arouse suspicion. He was sitting there thinking about her in ways he shouldn't while she was trying to confide in him. He was being an ass.

Camille eyed Remi skeptically for a moment and then said, "I'm actually done."

Good. Because he didn't need to hear any more. He rose from his seat, and threw some bills on the table. He then grabbed her hand, leading her out of the restaurant with her smaller hand firmly tucked into his larger one.

Chapter 6

Remington led her out of the restaurant and she had to nearly run to keep up with his long strides, courtesy of him being a foot taller than her. She mumbled a hasty goodbye to two of the sisters she saw on her way out. They smiled widely, though she knew they had the wrong idea about what was going on. Remi probably wanted to get her alone to ream her for making choices that had decided the course of his entire life.

He handed the valet his ticket and still didn't say a word as they waited for his car. She tried to mention that her car was there but he ignored her.

His face was unreadable and she didn't know whether to be scared or turned on by his controlling behavior right now. She felt like a character in one of her books being ordered to the secret room for her punishment.

Maybe Anna was right. Maybe she needed to get laid or something, just to get it out of the way because it was interfering with her sanity. She was in the middle of a confrontation ten years in the making, but couldn't get her mind off of the way Remi's slacks seemed to know exactly how to move with his muscled body and how the charcoal-gray material made her mouth water as it was the perfect casing for his perfect rear end.

When the car arrived Camille heard Remi tell the man to call a number on a card he'd scribbled on. He was arranging for her car to be taken care of. He asked for the ticket and she handed it to him without question.

He did the gentlemanly thing and opened the door for her. She got in and the seat seemed to form to her body. He entered on the other side and looked straight ahead for the duration of the hour-long drive. The only other time she'd seen him this intense was when his parents died. They'd been on a boating trip and never returned. His parents and two other couples were declared dead after parts of the vessel were found weeks after their disappearance. She hadn't been his girlfriend at the time but they'd been acquaintances and had attended the same church. It had been a terrible time for Remi and the town.

When they finally reached their destination Camille entered Remi's home hesitantly. She wasn't sure how she should behave right now since she didn't know what sort of mood Remi was in. He still had not given her a clue as to what was going on and why he was so quiet.

What I did wasn't that *big of a deal, was it?* .

She followed him through a cold-looking foyer with

marble flooring and white walls, down a long hall with several large rooms, and into a great room that had a contemporary-style bar at one end and all sorts of other seating in shades of white and gray. A large fish tank was the only color in the room as it glowed a brilliant blue and was teeming with vibrant fish.

Camille watched as Remi marched across the room. He looked as if he may have wanted to pour a drink but thought better of it. He then turned around just when she thought she'd go crazy if he didn't say *something*.

"Take off your clothes."

Not at all what she'd expected him to say.

Remi still wasn't showing any emotion and she didn't make a move to comply with his demand. She stood there and stared at him as if he'd lost his mind. There was no way she was going to…

Camille's thought slipped away when Remi started to stalk toward her with purpose. His beautifully sculpted muscles were tense and only now did she see the emotions warring within him. Lust, anger, love and hurt all battled for dominance but determination was the sentiment that seemed to win the war. He was very serious about his request, so she did what any warm-blooded American woman would do when presented with that request from an equally warm-blooded, sexy, virile, charming man who looked at her the way he did.

She stripped.

Am I really doing this? Should I tell him that this is my first time? Wasn't I just telling myself I needed to get laid and get over my little "obstacle"? Should I be remembering this so I can put it in one of my books?

Camille removed her clothing with the confidence of any character in her novels that had reached the point where the secrets and lies no longer mattered and they were ready to bare their soul, consequences be damned. However, she felt these consequences would be ones she'd thoroughly enjoy.

God, she was scared…and nervous.

Camille slowly peeled away the double-sided tape at her breasts, never taking her eyes off Remi. She then bared one smooth shoulder and then another. The stretchy fabric slid off of her, revealing perky, braless D-cup breasts.

Only looking away so she wouldn't fall as she stepped out of her dress, Camille pushed the expensive kelly-green fabric to the floor and kicked it aside after stepping out of it. She was the slightest bit afraid, turned on, embarrassed, anxious…but most of all she was completely drenched at the juncture of her thighs. No matter what this was about, Camille couldn't get past the fact that she was laid bare for him—literally—and completely at his mercy.

The idea made her stifle a moan of anticipation.

Remi had not spoken since his demand that she remove her clothing. He still didn't as he walked over to her. Standing before her, he assessed her, as if trying to figure out her every secret by just looking at her. She didn't flinch under his gaze even though she wanted to do so. She didn't know why he needed this, but he did. They both did. It was as if this act would make it official.

She'd returned to him.

He stared at her as if he could see the touch of every other man she'd been with, though she'd been with none. And then she remembered something he'd once said. He'd told her he'd lose it if she ever gave herself to another man before him. He'd said that he'd be able to look at her and tell, that it was something he wouldn't be able to handle because he loved her just that much. At the time, the statement had sounded barbaric and she'd laughed.

That was why he'd gone quiet. He was trying to figure out who and how many. He was doing what others did, except in a totally new and different way. The few who knew who she was, outside of Charlie and Anna, often looked at her as if they wanted to know if her books were based on reality. They weren't, but she'd never admit that. And Remi would never find that out by looking at her naked body. Though she was sure he had another mission in mind, as well.

"You left me, *Reese Elaine*," he said, and the name washed over her as if he'd whispered it against her skin. Rolling from his lips the name sounded different than when anyone else said it, and that turned her on more.

Camille took a deep, cleansing breath and said, "Yes. And I'd do it again if it meant protecting you."

"I see." Camille never thought two such words could free her of some of her guilt, but they had. It was as if he completely understood. Or maybe he had other things on his mind since his eyes now raked over her body, giving her a chill.

While lost in her brief thought Remi had moved close to her, and their bodies had aligned. Her eyes drifted upward taking in the hard plane of his chest before landing on the most intense brown eyes.

Forgiving eyes.

Was he upset? Yes. But would he hold it against her? No. She had done what she thought was best for them both. And as much as he wanted to say she was wrong, she wasn't. Her wanting to be a writer of erotic fiction would not have gone over well with his grandfather, the other members of the board of directors at Krane, or those who associated Krane Foods with a wholesome image. Neither would her career have gone over well in the political arena of such a religious town.

It pissed Remington off that people were so judgmental. It pissed him off that Camille had been about to give up her dream of being a writer to settle for being a teacher. While teaching was one of the most respectable jobs he could think of, it had not been her true dream.

The funny thing about it was that, even in her success, she was still protecting everyone. She'd chosen to write under a different name and not receive public accolades, just so she could protect her past, her hometown.

He could only imagine the kind of stress she'd been under at the time. He had only seen her once after her graduation before she left, and now that he looked back on that conversation, he could see why it had been a strained one. They'd discussed her upcoming plans to go to college in the city—the same one he had been commuting an hour to three days a week as he waited for her to finish high school.

He remembered she'd not been as enthusiastic as she had been in previous conversations and he thought that maybe she was just nervous about such a big change. But now he knew her mind had been preoccupied with the choice she'd already made.

Remi had no idea what came over him then. The idea of what she'd done to protect him—to protect them both—made him dizzy with admiration and desire. Her body—that delectably perfect body—called to him and made him want to show his appreciation in the most primitive way.

There was no point in being angry. She'd been an eighteen-year-old girl who was smart enough to make a sacrifice for them both, but in turn was able to pursue her dream. It had worked out and Remington couldn't deny that fact.

Except... He'd yet to tell her about his plans to run for mayor. That little nugget of information might put a wrench in any plan he had for them.

He actually hadn't told her much about himself yet, but he was sure they'd figure it out because Remi had already decided he wasn't letting Camille be the one doing the protecting. She'd returned to him and he wasn't going to lose her again.

It was his turn to protect her.

Which meant he had to come up with a plan to make sure she was committed to staying before she found out about his petition to run for mayor next year.

"I'm so sorry you had to make that decision," Remi proclaimed, moving past his thoughts and giving attention to his wants...and needs.

His lips placed soft kisses along her collarbone, up the column of her neck, and then he pulled back to stare at her beautiful face.

A soft trail of tears leaked from the corners of Camille's eyes and rolled down to her cheeks but she didn't take her eyes away from his. "*I'm* sorry. But I couldn't risk you possibly giving up anything for me and resenting me later or me resenting you."

Remi's mouth lowered to hers and he pressed his lips firmly to hers, reveling in the feel of her soft mouth responding to his. He groaned as matching warmth could be felt through the cloth of his pants, where the juncture of her legs rested against his thigh. He didn't care about the past hurt. All that mattered was that she was here now. She was with him. They'd deal with everything else later, together.

One hand came up to feel one full luscious breast at the very same time that his tongue sought entrance to her waiting mouth. Camille opened for him, her tongue matching the caresses and swirls of his own as they met in the simplest and most complicated of ways.

He lifted her up and carried her to his bedroom and laid her gently on the bed like the treasure she was. His heart rate picked up and his groin tightened when she smiled shyly at him as if she didn't write scenes just like this one for her books.

"Relax, Ladybug, I have you now." He had not used that nickname in more than ten years and the familiarity felt good.

Camille remembered the first time he'd used the variation of her father's nickname. He'd said she wasn't just any ordinary "bug." She was special and beautiful and brought him luck just like a ladybug.

Remi's hand crept slowly to her mound and pulled the flimsy thong aside. She was clean-shaven, allowing her moisture to seep unhindered over and between his long, exploring fingers. He had never felt a woman this wet for him, this ready. He briefly wondered if she was like this for any other man she'd been with and he had to push away thoughts of another man's hands on her because it made him want to break each and every one of their fingers for daring to touch what was his. Despite what he'd said in the past, his little assessment of her had not uncovered any clues as to whether she'd been touched by another man.

Camille caught his hesitation. "Is there something wrong, Remi?" she asked when he paused as the wayward thought came and went.

"No, Ladybug, I just… Your books…" He was being a jealous idiot, but she seemed to understand his hesitation.

"You're the only person I've ever desired—ever wanted to be with. I've never… I'm a virgin, Remi." Her face blushed and he released a sigh of relief. "My books…they are just stories plucked from my fantasies. Fantasies I've had about…you."

A low growl echoed throughout the bedroom. His erection pressed harder, begging to be released, his heart rate accelerated, and without knowing he was doing it he tore away the material hindering him from getting to her. His body lowered as he kissed his way down her heated skin. He was ravenous and only stopped for a moment to think about her confession before his face was at her mound, tasting her intimately and silently vowing that he'd be the only man to ever touch her this way.

Chapter 7

Camille couldn't believe she'd actually confessed to Remi that she had not had sex before. It was a relief and an embarrassment. But the way he responded had her body answering with excitement as the essence of her core trickled to the soft, fluffy duvet.

Two fingers taunted her wetness. They teased the aroused, swollen flesh of her nether regions, preparing her for what was to come. She sighed heavily when the two fingers were removed much too soon.

Remi brought the two moist digits to his mouth and sucked on them hard, not looking away from her. Camille's entire body shivered. She reached out for his belt and struggled to release it with their bodies so close.

Knowing she was having a hard time, he separated their bodies completely and stood over her. He removed his shirt, revealing a smooth chest with fine hairs that Camille couldn't wait to run her hands over to feel their downy softness. His pants were next and with them, he removed his underwear, if he was even wearing any at all.

There before her was his erection standing proud and twitching anxiously as if it were a piece of living art. She longed to reach out and touch it, taste it, feel it inside her, coax the waiting flow of semen out with the walls of her sex.

She didn't know what was happening and why she had these thoughts. She had not experienced such things and didn't know why she desired them now. It had to be Remington. She'd gone on dates and none of them had made it past first base. She'd never felt an inkling of what she was feeling now and didn't want to think about what that meant for her.

"Stand up. Let me look at you. I need to see you again knowing you're about to be mine," Remi said when he was naked. She thought that she should be the one saying that to him. The man was walking sin!

As she stood, what was left of her underwear fell down to the floor. She stood there in only her heels, feeling quite sexy as his gaze raked over her as if making love to her with his eyes.

Once he'd gotten his fill, he took a step in her direction. His hands drifted up her arms slowly, purposefully and her head lolled back, inviting him in for more. As his hands ascended her arms, her hands moved to his chest. Solid muscle provoked her fingers to further inspection. The tactile sensation of her skin against his was heady to say the least and at the most, it was orgasm-inducing.

Remi's lips pressed into her hairline as his hands moved up and into her tousled locks. He was taking his time and she loved it. She felt just like one of the heroines in her books that were first treated tenderly until the hero rode the innocent girl hard, divesting her of innocence.

"I'm going to make love to you, Camille. And then I'm going to take you…hard. Do you understand?" he asked and she could only nod because his words were like hot lava pouring over her virginal body.

Remi didn't waste any time. He barely let her finish nodding before he scooped her up and wrapped her legs around his waist. Their mouths met in a frenzy of lips and tongues vying for a place to lick and suck, touch and kiss.

"Oh, I need you, Remi." Camille meant it with every fiber of her being. She wanted this man to be the one to end her self-imposed abstinence. She wanted him to be inside her and show her all the things she'd been missing.

It was all he needed to hear, apparently. Remington moaned her name and attacked her mouth once again. He lowered her to the bed and climbed above her. His tongue darted out and licked its way down her body as if she was the tastiest lollipop in the candy store. His mouth moved to her core and latched on without preamble, sucking and kissing away the never-ending stream of moisture. His fingers dipped into her core when his teeth grazed her pearl, and her hips rose at the delicious feeling.

"Ohhhh, Remi…"

"Don't hold back on me, Ladybug. I want to hear you screaming for me."

Remi treated the lips of her core just like the lips of her mouth as he kissed her there and swirled his skilled tongue around her hardened nub. The resulting orgasm gradually built up in intensity the longer he laved at her and she rode the soft wave of her release. It was a great start to what she knew would be a memorable night.

Camille had not gotten over the first orgasm when the sound of foil tearing penetrated her brain. And then Remi was entering her, without any further preparation, only a mumbled warning. She'd expected it to hurt more than it did, but the pain quickly subsided due to his skilled distractions, leaving more a full feeling rather than any sort of pain. It was…glorious, or maybe Remi just knew what he was doing.

In and out he drove into her, rhythmically and gently, causing her moans to reach a pitch Camille didn't know she could achieve. When he'd finally coaxed her open fully, he drove himself into the hilt and he sighed. It was as if he'd been holding back for her comfort. He then plunged deep and began to leave gentle behind in exchange for staking a passionate claim on her with his forceful thrusts. And she loved it.

"Mine! You. Are. Mine!"

Remington Krane had just claimed this woman as if he was some animal. He declared her as his and he did not regret saying it. This woman, whom he was in love with, had not been sullied by the touch of another man and he knew he wouldn't be too arrogant in saying that she was waiting for this moment. Somewhere inside her she'd known this day would come and she'd waited for him.

"Yes!" she said in response to his declaration. But he didn't need her approval. He was letting her know that no man would have her for as long as he had breath in his body. She'd saved her body for him and the thought made him want to ditch the barrier and claim her in a way he shouldn't.

The rhythm continued as he poured his soul into her. His head was buried in her neck and their bodies were melded together as if one being. He mumbled incoherently about how much he loved her and thought about her all these years they were apart.

His words sparked something in her and she started to thrust her hips against his. She seemed to want this round of lovemaking to be rough and crude, but Remi was not complaining at all. He took the upward thrust of her hips as an invitation and began slamming into her vigorously.

"I'm not hurting you, am I?" he panted between thrusts.

"No. More. Please, Remington."

He gave Camille more of him. He flipped their positions with little effort. Their bodies never disconnected and before he knew it he had her straddling his hips, giving her more. The new position pushed him deeper into her wetness. His hands found her breasts and then trailed down her curvy sides until they settled on the flare of her hips. He held her there exulting in her tightness, her warmth, her scent, her beauty, her…*everything*.

And then she started to move above him.

This woman—this inexperienced woman—rode him like a lover possessed. Her hips swerved in figure-eight motions, her hands gripped his chest muscles, and her toes curled against his thighs. And the sounds… The sounds coming from her were like music to his ears. His eyes closed as he savored the feel of her on top of him, controlling him, loving him.

His hips thrust up, nearly knocking her off him and making them both laugh through their lust. She held on and met each of his thrusts as if she was practiced at this. Finding the cheeks of her rear, Remi squeezed and separated them pushing him deeper until the tip of his erection grazed that soft, spongy part of her, igniting her excited release.

Camille screamed out, throwing her head back as she chanted his name into the room around them. As she came, her walls milked him, until finally, he broke into a million tiny pieces, finding his own powerful release.

It was so forceful that when it passed, he sat straight up and threw his arms around her to make sure this wasn't some vivid dream.

"Oh. My. Goodness!" Camille exclaimed. He could feel her sweat-slicked body and her rapid heart pounding in her chest. "That was… I don't even know how to explain it since I haven't had any experience, but this is one for the books…literally," Camille declared and laughed at the double meaning of her words. He didn't mind. It was flattering to know that she thought his performance worthy of her adoring fans.

"You might have enough ideas for several books once I'm done with you," Remi admitted, and then pulled her to him. He kissed her deeply and passionately until his semihard member grew inside her once again. "Turn over. I'm not done with you yet," Remi whispered against her ear and she did as he requested.

Camille had no idea that real people could actually have that many orgasms in one night. She'd heard Anna mention her multiple orgasms, but always thought the woman was exaggerating.

She wasn't exaggerating.

Camille was exhausted and muscles ached in her that she didn't know existed. Her legs felt like jelly, her body was satiated and her smile was never-ending. She stretched and felt the hard body next to her stir from his slumber.

"I thought you'd be long gone, but I'm happy you have no regrets."

"None at all." Camille rose, taking the sheet with her. He protested the sudden departure of his covers as it left him naked. Camille padded across the room to the bathroom they'd christened sometime during the night. "I'm taking a bath if you'd like to join me," Camille invited and Remi didn't hesitate to join.

Hours later, their bodies wrinkled from the tub, they both sat in Remi's state-of-the-art chef's kitchen. Camille tugged at the humongous lounge pants Remi had lent her and for the hundredth time, tried to keep her right breast from popping out the side of the men's tank top undershirt she wore.

"It's time for breakfast," Remi told her, nodding at the clock. "Scrambled eggs, no cheese…grits, bacon, hash browns and toast. Is that still your favorite breakfast?"

"Not sure. I don't think I've had grits since I lived here and I can't remember the last time I had all those items on the same plate."

"Well then it will be my honor to make you a good old country breakfast. Oh, and your phone rang while you were drying your hair. Charlie, I think."

Camille had forgotten to call Charlie back last night. She was supposed to tell him how the meeting with her distributor had gone. At least he knew she'd been with Remi. She had not told him about the gift Remi had sent or the invitation to dinner, even though she'd intended to ask for her friend's advice on all that. She guessed it was a little too late for that since…well, she'd already made her decision and where it all went from here was beyond her comprehension right now. She was enjoying a moment with a lost love and where that moment took them had yet to be discovered. She'd enjoy the ride until it was time to return to her real life back in New York because she had no delusions about this being anything more than sex, regardless of how many feelings and emotions were involved.

After a meal that was even bigger than he'd promised, Camille was tired and ready to return to bed until she realized what day it was. It was Monday. People who didn't write for a living had to actually arrive at an office, and she was holding up the man who ran the entire damn company.

"Am I keeping you from work? I didn't mean to. I can just— Oh, God…Daddy. I bet he's worried sick!"

"He's not worried—at least not anymore. I called him this morning to let him know you were okay. He was worried a little since he hadn't heard from you. I think Reese needs you more than he's willing to admit."

Camille was so used to being on her own that she had a hard time remembering to check in with her father. "Dammit. I have to call him."

"He knew you'd say that and he said to tell you not to bother. He said he was going to have one of the church members take him over to the rec center to walk the track like the doctor prescribed. He told me not to let you come running home."

"Oh…well, I guess I'm all yours today."

Remi smiled at her words and came closer. He leaned in, planting the sweetest of kisses on her lips. "I like the sound of that. And I run the company so I can go in to work when I want," Remi said responding to her earlier inquiry.

She'd been so busy completing writing obligations yesterday that she'd forgotten her father had fired the nurse and no one was at home with him. She had to do better. She had not come back to Fairdell for Remington Krane and that would be obvious when she returned to her real life—in New York.

"I need to go. I need to check on my father. I— Where's my car?"

"I had it taken back to the rental place here in town.

You can go sign the paperwork later. And like I said, your father is fine." The look on Remi's face suggested there was something more to what he said, but she let it go. But she'd still call her father and check on him for her own peace of mind. "Granddad had a blockage and was back on his feet in a week," Remi reassured her. "I'm sure your dad will rebound quickly."

"Well, at least I don't have to do the walk of shame. I think it would've been ten times worse with my father home."

"Can you write from anywhere? I mean any city in the world?" he asked and she was surprised at the sudden change in subject matter.

His question caught her off guard. She didn't know what he was getting at and she didn't ask. She gave the most precise answer she could muster. "Yes."

He nodded and then continued to clear the dishes from the small kitchen table. Her second offer to help was denied and so she sat at the table waiting for him to finish his task as a pensive expression overtook his features. He seemed to tuck away the thought for a later date. She looked at him for a moment to see if he might elaborate and when he didn't, she got up and made her way to his room to retrieve her dress, shoes and bag.

"I should head out," she said when she returned to the kitchen, the clothes in her hand. "I—I have to call my agent and follow up with her about the dinner meeting last night. I don't want to rock the boat before I get the deal and… I'm not good at this, Remington." She took a deep breath. "Actually, I have no experience at this at all. I don't know how this day-after thing goes so…" She pointed over her shoulder. "Can you, uh… I need a ride home."

Chapter 8

She was practically flapping around like a fish out of water as she tried to figure out how to deal with the infamous "morning after." He stood there staring because her floundering was adorable. So adorable that his pants started to tighten as his manhood swelled at the sight of her in his oversize clothing.

He decided to put her out of her misery, but not in the way she thought. She continued to talk and then he grabbed her around her waist and pulled her to him. The noise she emitted was a mix between a squeal and a moan.

"There is nothing…I mean *nothing* about this moment that should be awkward." The back of his knuckles grazed the side of her face and she leaned into his hand. "There will be no walk of shame, Ladybug. I wasn't just caught up in the moment when I said I love you. I have *always* loved you. You are mine. I meant that too when I said it."

He hoped the look he gave her echoed his words. He hoped the question he asked her about her work location had her thinking. He hoped…he hoped a lot of things. But most of all he hoped that Camille was back in Fairdell to stay…with him. He hoped that when she learned about his plans to pursue a political career, she'd remember the night they spent together and the words he just said.

He lowered his head and captured her lips, demanding she part hers and offer herself up to him for a little morning exploration. He caressed more than he kissed, lightly devouring her but holding her tightly in his arms. Their tongues tangled and only when they needed to breathe did Remi pull away, leaving one lingering kiss on her forehead.

"Come on, let's go," Remi said and she stood there staring at him, clutching her clothes. He was trying not to take it personally that Camille had not said anything in response to his declaration of love. He understood she needed time to catch up to him. "You have a driver now so you don't need your rental anymore." Remi smiled triumphantly at his plan to spend as much time with Camille as possible.

She laughed and shook her head as she followed him out. He loved the sound of her throaty giggle. It reminded him of some of the little sounds she emitted when they made love.

Remi found himself with an overwhelming need to

touch her. He placed a hand on her hip as they crossed
the driveway of his home that sat on a few acres on the
outskirts of town. She giggled again when he squeezed
her backside and fell into his chest playfully. They were
just about to kiss again when his grandfather's driver
pulled up.

"Do you know who that is, Rem?"

"You calling me 'Rem' now, huh?" She used to call
him that all the time so this meant her comfort level was
returning. She was about to speak but he said, "Hold
that thought…"

Camille couldn't believe how much her demeanor
had changed in twenty-four hours. She was actually
giggling with a man, flirting and having sex…multiple
times. For the moment she didn't have a worry; she was
simply trying to enjoy Remington Krane and not think
about the future or what his longing gazes or odd questions were about.

She was on cloud nine with Remington. She was so
wrapped up in him that she had not even realized she
was still in his clothes and that her hair was probably
standing up all over her head from being without her
satin pillowcase. Nor did she hear the car until it had
stopped in front of them. She hoped the person in the
vehicle was no one too important, though she was sure
it was since it looked to her like a hired car.

Hopes are just that…hopes. Because the window
to the limo lowered and she saw who it was. Frederick
Krane. He was the only man who'd have a driver shuf-
fle him around town. He was an impossible snob and

he hated her with a passion. She thought it ironic how he treated her as if she was beneath him even though he called himself a man of faith.

"Good morning, Mr. Krane," Camille said very sweetly. "Nice to see you again."

"Ms. Ryan. I had no idea you were in town. Remi never mentioned you. Wonder why that is?" The old man then turned his attention to Remi. "I came by to take you to lunch. The Brandts will be meeting us there."

It was hard for Camille to stifle a groan at the man's antics. *Is he still on this?* She couldn't remember a time when Frederick Krane had not endorsed Sonya Brandt as a potential life mate for Remington. The Brandts were another one of the wealthy families in town, but where Mr. Krane was a hard, evil man, Sonya's father and her grandfather were virtual teddy bears in comparison. The Brandts to watch out for were the women, because they could control the men with one simple upset moment. They were the female counterparts to Frederick Krane and were just as determined as he to get what they wanted.

Mr. Krane cleared his throat. "But I can see that you are otherwise…*occupied.*" At that word, the old man's gaze landed on Camille and she tried to wrap her arms even tighter around her body. She felt not only as if she needed to shield herself from being seen in the literal sense being that she was braless, but also dirty and cheap because of that one word. It was amazing that Frederick Krane could do that to her so easily.

Remi stepped forward. "Yes, Granddad, I am occupied so I won't be going with you to lunch. Please give the Brandts my regards and my apologies. I already have plans for the day with Camille." Remi was standing close to the window. Camille suspected he was trying to block her from the old man's view and she was grateful for that. She had no idea what *plans* he spoke of but she didn't care at the moment if it would get the old man to leave.

"Yes, I see," said the elder Krane. "I guess a man needs to sow his oats before he finds someone suitable. I'll be on my way, then." He didn't give Remi a chance to defend Camille. His automatic window rolled up and the car pulled away from a fuming Remi.

Camille walked the few steps to close the distance between her and Remi. "It's okay. I'm older and a lot less sensitive than I was in the old days. I know that some people are set in their ways. Which is why I kept Reese Elaine a secret." She said the last part under her breath. She had a feeling that people in town would see her as Remi's grandfather did if and when they found out who she really was.

This would be a disaster. She had to tell her father before he was blindsided because in Fairdell nothing ever remained a secret. Once one person found out a secret, someone else was bound to find out. It was inevitable. She should've stayed away, but there was no way she wouldn't have come home to see her sick father.

"I'd never tell anyone about Reese Elaine." Remi wrapped her in his arms and she looked up at him. "But I'd love it if one day soon you were ready to reveal your secret."

That was definitely a hint to something more. However, thoughts of what he could possibly mean made her stomach quiver with unease.

Remington brought the car to a stop at the red light, and let his mind wander back over the morning. He'd had some time to think before Camille woke. After Remi had talked to her father and her father had mentioned that Charlie was worried about Camille, he'd had an idea.

Of course he'd realized he needed to be friends with Charlie, which was why he'd gone to see him. Not only had he wanted to find out about Camille and why she'd left, he'd also wanted the blessing of her best friend.

Remington could admit that he and Charlie had never got along well. He was never enthusiastic about Camille's best friend being a guy. And it didn't help that Remi and Charlie had hung out with the same set of boys from being on high school teams together. Remington's friends had often questioned him about how he put up with Camille being so close to another guy. He could rarely answer because he didn't know how to tell his peers that he tolerated their friendship because he loved Camille and trusted her. He doubted a group of teenage boys would have understood the depth of his feelings.

However, Remi thought Camille should be aware that he was trying with Charlie. He wanted her to know so she could prepare herself. He planned to work his way into every aspect of her life so it would be hard for her to give him up again. If it meant striking up a friendship with Charlie, then so be it. The man would have to get used to Remington because he planned to be in Camille's life, one way or another, even if it meant chasing her to New York if she tried to run from him again.

But would he be able to convince her to stay? Remington's confidence level had been shockingly high since he woke that morning. He knew Camille and knew she wouldn't have slept with him just for sex. She wasn't that type. He was sure there was more to their lovemaking even if she had not realized it yet.

His grandfather stopping by showed he may have a harder time getting through to her than he'd thought that morning. He saw the way she shied away from his grandfather and didn't defend herself when he made some negative insinuations. She may be more confident as the writer Reese Elaine, current resident of New York, but back home she was still the daughter of a single father. She was still the girl who'd broken a boy's heart. And if these people—the people he loved so dearly—found out about what she did for a living, *they* may be the ones to make her flee, not him and the secret he was keeping from her.

"I told you I went to see Charlie and that's how I found you." As the light changed, Remington glanced over at Camille to see if she was listening since she didn't answer. He figured she was waiting to see where he was going with this since she already knew how he'd found her last night. "I not only went to see him to find out why you left—which he didn't tell me—but I also wanted him to know how I feel about you." Remington could see Camille shift in her seat out of the corner of his eye. She might not be prepared to hear this yet, but she'd better get ready because she wasn't leaving him again.

"Rem, please don't—"

"No, Camille. Listen to me. I went to Charlie because I know you love him and you care what he thinks. He and I aren't the best of friends, but I had to tell him that I want you and plan to have you."

"You said that to Charlie and he didn't punch you?"

Remington smiled. She was joking so she hadn't panicked because of his words. Or maybe she wasn't joking. Charlie was as protective as her father, so maybe the man truly believed Remington cared for Camille, which was why he hadn't demanded Remi stay away from Camille. That meant Charlie was on his side.

The thought that this tentative plan of his may actually work relaxed Remi. He was still worried about how she'd react when she found out he was running for mayor, but by that time she'd be his fiancée and he'd have a plan to make sure their small Bible-thumping town didn't try to crucify Camille when they found out how she earned her money.

"I've been going over this condition my dad had and I've even done a little research. He may feel better, but…"

Her words trailed off when she saw him sitting there in her family home staring at her as she struggled to put on one of her shoes. He'd offer to help, but he couldn't stop staring at her. She was beautiful as a girl, but as a woman there was a grace and femininity about her that commanded attention. She was more than beautiful, she was stunning.

She'd changed into a white dress that stopped midthigh, giving way to long brown legs. The dress was snugly fitted to her body and she had downplayed it with a pair of floral printed laceless canvas shoes, yet she still held herself like a stylish woman of twenty-eight. She had tossed a light sweater on the ottoman in front of him that looked as if it could fit a toddler. The sight of her caused him to grin devilishly as he thought about her small body wrapped around him, controlling him as if *he* was the smaller one.

She bent down again to put on her shoe, the curve of her rear hiking into the air, and he groaned. This sight was doing a number on Remington's sanity. The sexiest part about it was that she had no idea how she affected him.

"You okay?" Camille said hesitantly, seemingly cautious of his silence.

"Fine, Ladybug. Just waiting for you. What were you saying about your father?" Remington recovered and rose from his seat to get away from thoughts of throwing her on the ottoman and burying himself deep inside her. She needed time to recover since it had been her first time. And while he'd been a selfish bastard the night before, he'd let her mend properly before he allowed himself to have her again. He just needed to have some control.

Remi wiped his hand down his face and stepped to the window. He was once again reminded of times he'd spent at this house as a teenager. The nostalgia calmed his raging libido enough for him to face Camille again.

"I was going to ask if there was a food delivery service in the area you could recommend." She started to straighten the few items that were out of place and he couldn't take his eyes off her as she moved. Cleaning, straightening and organizing were things she used to do to keep her hands busy as she talked or listened when they were younger. It was cute to see she still had the habit. "Daddy won't buy healthy food for himself so I figure if I have— Remi, why are you staring at me like that?"

He'd been caught.

Chapter 9

She'd described that look, she'd researched that look, she'd watched movies and videos to know what that expression could mean. But never did Camille think it could be so real or directed at her. But this was real. Remi was real. And his eyes told her that he wanted her. And she'd be damned if she didn't want him as well even though the insistent throbbing at her core said she wasn't quite ready to have him again.

"I know your dad was going for a walk, but is your father's nurse here?" Remington asked. Before she could answer, he moved toward her.

"Fired."

They weren't touching, but she felt a distinctive magnetism, as if something was forcing them to close the final distance. Remington's head lowered at the same time his hand cupped Camille's hip softly. The comforting feel of his touch forced a sigh from her lips.

Her hands found Remington's arms and held on as his fingers played with the hem of her dress. She braced herself so she wouldn't fall over backward as his kiss forced her head to tilt back and her to go up on her toes.

He seemed to sense her distress and used his other hand to anchor her at her lower back. Not realizing she was being lowered, Camille gasped when the padded chair-sized ottoman grazed her back.

"I don't think we should—" Camille's protest was cut off by her own moan. Remington had such skilled fingers and when he slid her panties aside and dipped his finger into her, there were no more words or protests she could utter.

One lingering kiss to her lips and a mischievous smile was all he gave her in warning before he lowered himself with the grace of a gazelle going after its prey. Spreading her knees wide and lifting her legs to his shoulders, Remington's head disappeared between her thighs. She gasped at the feel of his nose as it grazed the slit of her opening through the scant satin fabric.

Camille wasn't sure if she should stop this. No, she knew she should stop this, but the sheer pleasure of the moment rendered her incapable of rational thought. Before she knew what was happening, her panties were being lowered and his tongue was devouring her core.

His lips explored her voraciously in the most intimate of kisses and his tongue stroked her most sensitive spot. His fingers dipped and delved into her, stroking her deeply and igniting her to a most unexpected release.

She breathed heavily and slapped at him to move away from her when she could take no more, but he continued to lap at her, causing her body to shake with mini orgasms as he got his fill of her.

Remington kissed the inside of her thigh and Camille smiled. She couldn't believe this was what her first sexual experiences were like. She'd heard horror stories and was glad she wasn't among those whose first time had been forgettable. It was easy to see Remington knew what he was doing, which also begged the question of who he'd been doing it with all these years. If his grandfather so easily brought up the Brandts in front of her, did that mean Remi had been seeing Sonya?

"Are you sleeping with Sonya?"

The question was unexpected even on Camille's end. She snapped her mouth closed for fear something else she'd wanted to think instead of say would pass her lips.

Maybe it was seeing Frederick Krane and his mention of the Brandts that had caused her slip, but his grandfather's invite to lunch had been at the back of her mind since they'd seen him.

Camille knew it was unfair of her to question Remington since she lived out of town and planned to return to New York, but she needed to know. Sonya lived in town and was the lawyer for Krane Foods. Camille wondered if the woman had earned that position or if it was one of the perks of sleeping with the boss.

Hating the direction of her thoughts, but holding firm to wanting to know the answer to her question, Camille tried to back away from the intimate position she and Remi were in. Remington halted her, gently pulling the hem of her dress back into place and then helping her into a seated position. They shared a look that was intimate and personal, which added to all of the other intimate, personal moments they'd shared in the past hours.

Whereas Camille had once thought of this reunion as closure, she now realized she wasn't built that way. She couldn't sleep with Remington and not be stirred into wanting more. She'd fooled herself into thinking this could possibly be a onetime act since every time he looked at her or touched her she was reminded of the dreams she'd had of one day returning to Remi and sharing this kind of passion.

So her question was a valid one. If she was going to open herself up to him while she was here, she wouldn't share him or be in the dark about some on-again, off-again relationship he shared with Sonya Brandt.

Are you sleeping with Sonya?

What kind of question was that to pose after what he'd just done?

Remi wasn't sure of the answer, but he'd known this would come up after his grandfather's mention of the Brandts. Of course Camille remembered the family whom she often had to concede to on the days his grandfather insisted he go to the country club or attend some function for his business friends.

The Brandts and the Kranes were close. Remington's father and Sonya's had been really good friends before his parents were lost to him. Afterward his grandfather had maintained the relationship. Their families attended the same church, held the same political affiliations and had mutual business associates. And Remington had been raised around Sonya and her brother.

It had been practically an unwritten arrangement that he and Sonya would be married one day as if it was what he wanted. His mother and hers had always talked about the day when their families would be "officially" related. It wasn't until Remington truly became interested in dating that his mother and father accepted he wasn't going to be with Sonya. However, Fredrick Krane was not as moved by Remington's free will.

Remington had to admit that Camille was strong because Sonya hadn't been an easy girl to deal with back then. Sonya had often made sure to remind Camille what his grandfather thought of Camille and her father. Any other girl probably would have left Remi alone, but not Camille. She had put up with Sonya without making it an issue in their relationship. She'd never allowed Remington to be rude to Sonya and had never asked him to tell her to back off. She was confident in their relationship, which was why he still didn't understand why she had run. They could've dealt with her wanting to be a writer—maybe.

Remington shook that thought off and focused on Camille's question. "No, I am not sleeping with Sonya. I have never been in a relationship with her, but…"

"You slept with her," Camille finished when he trailed off.

"Yes. A few months after you left. She caught me in a bad place, not that it is an excuse. I—"

"No need to explain. I left you without a word or

note. I can't be upset about it, I just needed…I needed to know just in case I have to see her."

Remington did not want to dwell on talk of Sonya, so he changed the subject. He still lay on top of her on the ottoman as he asked, "Did you want to make those calls? You mentioned your agent and some meeting you had to do a follow-up on…"

"I'll call them but first you need to tell me what it is you have planned, Mr. Krane. What is all this you were telling your grandfather about already having plans with me?" She flashed a flirty smile at him and he felt his manhood perk up at the simple gesture.

"How about a date?"

She hesitated and he wondered if she'd try and back out of being with him today. He'd already told her he loved her and he didn't even care that she had not said it back. He could wait. But he wouldn't wait long. He'd do anything he could to make her face her feelings and admit she loved him, as well. He'd help her through her guilt over leaving him. If he wasn't angry, she had no reason to be reluctant about a relationship between them.

"Are you sure about that? It's one thing to be doing this," Camille said and gestured back and forth between them, "but you do know how the people of this town feel about me in regards to you? They think I made a fool of you…and I'd have to agree with them so you may not want to—"

"I want to. I don't care what they think." Remi placed one hand at the nape of Camille's neck and ran the other over her thick hair and stroked tenderly. He then tilted her chin up with his thumb and hoped she could see what he felt for her in his eyes. He'd confessed a lot, but he'd give her more time to come to terms with what he already knew—she was his and she wasn't leaving him again.

She pulled away from him and said, "What are we doing here, Remi…really?" He was losing her to her doubts. He was sure she was afraid that, even years later, the circumstances that had taken her away from him were *still* going to keep them apart and that scared her. Remi just thanked God that she hadn't asked if he still wanted to pursue his political career. He didn't want to lie to her, but she wasn't ready for that truth just yet.

He had to first make her see what she'd missed while they were apart. He needed to show her that he hadn't changed—they hadn't changed. He decided to take her out the way he used to and she was in town at the perfect time to do that. "I'm winning you over," he answered. He gave her a wink. "Freshen up and then I'm showing you off."

"Where are we going, Rem?" Camille asked very sweetly as if that would make him talk. He wasn't talking. Because if he did, she'd surely back out.

Half an hour later, he whipped his black Maserati into a parking space and hopped out the car before she could ask him any questions. He strode over to her side to help her out and thought how right she looked taking his hand to head out for an afternoon together. This was the way it should've been. It could be that way again, he told himself. He just had to convince her that she could live in Fairdell *and* be Reese Elaine. He'd stand by her, her father would stand by her, and she'd be surprised how many people in their town would not crucify her or criticize her for doing a job she loved—at least that's what he hoped. It didn't matter what she wrote about. She was a bestselling author and her star would only shine brighter if she were to come out from behind her alias.

When she got out of the car, she looked around. He could tell she was hesitant but he confidently took her hand and laced their fingers together.

"What is this?" Camille whispered under her breath and it was obvious that she wasn't happy that he'd brought her to such a public place. They were downtown on the square, Remington explained, in the midst of A Taste of Fairdell, the annual event he'd started recently, where residents and restaurants set up tasting booths. The proceeds from the ticket sales went to the local food pantry for families in need. It was an endeavor Krane Foods had taken on under Remington's leadership and guidance.

"How are they doing this in the middle of the day?" she asked. "Aren't people at work or at school?"

"Well, they do this every day at lunch for a week, from about eleven to two in the afternoon. Then on the weekend the booths stay open all day. There are performances, raffles, face painting…you know, one last hurrah before the kids get too deep into the school year. A way to say goodbye to summer."

He was glad that she looked impressed by what his company was doing in their small town, but he hated that she tensed as they received stares from people as they walked by. He could see that Camille pretended not to notice, but what she failed to realize was that people probably didn't recognize her. If anything, they were staring because Remi was with a woman—a woman they didn't seem to know or recognize. They'd be surprised to know this was Cammie, the girly tomboy who was her father's shadow and Remi's long-time girlfriend from years past. *He* sometimes had to look at her twice to make sure it was really her. She'd grown into quite a beautiful woman with curves, intelligence and a face he was sure got lots of attention from adoring males and jealous females.

Camille didn't doubt that this whole event was for a good cause. She'd been to a similar fair one summer in Chicago and had enjoyed herself immensely. However, she couldn't say the same today since people were staring. She knew they felt a little miffed with her for the way she'd left Remi all those years ago but if he didn't have a problem with her return, then neither should anyone else. Camille decided to ignore the stares. She'd think of herself as Reese Elaine, the confident, best-selling author.

"You know they have no idea who you are, right?"

She turned to Remi. "What do you mean? *Everyone* is staring… Why would they be staring if they didn't know who I was?" After all, she'd been a resident of Fairdell for the first seventeen years of her life. There was no reason why people shouldn't recognize her, despite the fact that her visits had been brief and few over the years.

Remi stopped in front of a store and pulled her under the shaded overhang, out of the walkway. He turned her so that he was blocking her from view and then took her sunglasses off her face and held them up to her. "This is why. Some might've known, but I have a feeling that this has to do with them thinking that I have decided to take up with some outsider instead of getting a 'nice' woman from Fairdell." He chuckled. "Little do they know, I have the nicest and most beautiful of souls with me today." He then leaned in and kissed her right below her ear and she shivered, the kiss reminding her of their exploits from the previous night and that morning. "I want you to relax. You're here with me and I'm the most powerful man in Fairdell."

The statement was arrogant but not in a condescending way. He didn't look down on the people of their town; he was simply stating a fact. Being the president and CEO of the company that provided lots of jobs for the city, being the sexiest man in the city and being a Krane made him undoubtedly the most powerful man from Fairdell to Atlanta. Krane was a huge company and had been around since before Remington's parents were born.

"Okay, I'll try. You ready to feed me? Because I'm hungry."

He took a deep breath as if her words meant more than what she'd intended. He then placed a hand on the wall behind her and she felt small with him hovering over her. He was poised to attack her in the most sensual way, but they were in public and she was already on the bad side of most of the townspeople. A public spectacle like this would just cement their opinions of her. She didn't care what it meant for her, but she did care what it meant for her father and his reputation, as well as Remi's.

Remi must've read her thoughts because just as he was about to pounce on her lips, he pulled away. "We should probably get going so I can…feed you. You and that dress are doing something to me right now and if we don't get out of here someone might use this scene against me when— Never mind. Let's go."

Remi then grabbed her hand and they continued their stroll along the square, not letting her respond to his last statement. She wanted to ask what he was about to say, but he pulled her away too quickly so she shrugged it off for now.

They passed a few booths before Remi stopped at a ticketing counter and picked up enough tickets to feed five people.

Chapter 10

"Bug...? Is that you?" Camille knew that was the voice of her father coming from behind her. She smiled and then let go of the firm hold Remi had on her hand and hugged her father.

"Why didn't you tell me you wanted to get out of the house today? I would've made sure to be home to take you." She knew Remi had told her that her father had someone to take him where he needed to go, but she hadn't expected to see him out with a woman.

"I talked to Remington and he said he'd tell you. I didn't want to interrupt your *fun*," her father said suggestively and she rolled her eyes. She and her father were close enough that they could joke about things like their dates. He often tried to explain to her that the women he'd made "friends" with over the years could never replace her mother, but he was a man and he had needs. Camille may not have liked the fact that her father had dated a few of the women in town, but there was no way she'd object. She'd never told him but she'd always felt as if it was her fault that he was alone and that if she'd never been born then he and her mother would be living happily ever after.

"Oh, please, Daddy. You know I would've dropped everything for you," she said and then looked over her shoulder at Remi. He held his hands up in mock surrender.

"I was just doing as I was told. Your father insisted I didn't bother you." Remi made his way closer to her side, taking her hand in his once again. Her father smiled at the gesture and Camille then turned her attention to the woman beside her father who seemed to be getting tired of being ignored.

"Hello. I'm Camille." She extended her hand to the woman who introduced herself as Ms. Savage. She had light brown skin, light brown eyes, a neat, shoulder-length hairstyle, and was dressed casually in a modest A-line skirt and matching top. The woman was above average in beauty, but the slight scowl she flashed Camille when she and Remi linked hands turned Camille completely off.

"So nice to meet you. Your father is always talking about his 'Bug'," she said, and it didn't sound like she was too happy to meet Camille. It was the first direct display of hostility toward her besides what she'd gone through with Remi's grandfather.

"She's right, Bug. I am proud of my baby girl for

going out and making something of herself. I tell everyone about how successful you are in New York," her father said proudly.

Camille's stomach turned at the words from her father. She was lying to him and he did nothing but give her the utmost praise and adoration. Remi must've noticed her blanching and squeezed her hand as a show of support. She felt better but that still didn't excuse her lies. She'd have to tell her father and hope that he would not be too disappointed in her. He was the only one she wanted to please and his approval meant the world to her.

The group talked a little more about the event and whom they'd seen so far. The conversation prepared her for who she might see while they were at the food fair, but it didn't prepare her for the invitation Ms. Savage extended to a dinner at a home Camille technically owned. There was no doubt the woman was letting Camille know of her claim on Reese Ryan and she confirmed that when she mentioned *she'd* invited Charlie to the dinner *she'd* be hosting. Camille didn't say a word in protest and felt she was adult enough to handle one evening with the woman.

"Oh, and Mr. Krane, we'd be honored if you'd join us, as well. There will be plenty to go around. I have no qualms about cooking for three gorgeous men!"

Camille had a feeling that this woman was going to be trouble. She'd already been giving Camille sideways glances and she wasn't sure if the woman didn't like her because of the attention she got from her father or if it was that she'd been drinking the same "hate Camille Kool-Aid" the rest of the town had been sipping. It was probably both.

"I'd like that," Remi said, "if Camille doesn't mind."

Camille had been caught up in her thoughts. The woman made her paranoia return after Remington had helped her through it just a few minutes ago. She was looking around now, noticing the scathing glances from the women and covetous ones from the men. "Huh?" she said when she heard her name mentioned.

"Dinner. Ms. Savage invited me. You don't mind if I—"

"Of course she doesn't, Mr. Krane, and please call me Bernice."

"Well, in that case please call me Remi. But we really should get going. I want to show Camille around a little if you don't mind."

"Oh…sorry to hold you guys up," her father said. "I'll see you at home, Bug. Do you need anything while I'm out?"

"Daddy, you were the one in the hospital and you're asking *me* if I need anything?" Camille shook her head at him. "I'm fine. You and Ms. Savage go ahead and enjoy the rest of the day." Camille turned to Bernice Savage and put on her most charming smile. "Please make sure he takes it easy. He has the tendency to—"

"Don't you worry about him, Camille. I have it under control."

Camille just stared at the woman for a moment before her father pulled Bernice away. He gave Camille a sympathetic look over his shoulder as they walked in the direction that she and Remi had just come from.

"See what I mean?" Camille said when she and Remi started to walk again. "People can't help themselves. They think it's okay to be that way to me. It's not right. They think they can judge me for leaving when they have no idea why I left."

"I'm sorry."

"Why are *you* sorry?" Camille stopped again and looked up at Remi, wondering what he could be sorry about. "You're the one person that should be able to judge me for what I did and—"

"I forgave you the moment you left. No point in wallowing in anger when I could spend that time loving you." He lifted their joined hands and kissed Camille's knuckles. "I never stopped loving you, Camille. Out of sight does not mean out of mind. You were on my mind each and every day, but I respected your wishes not to contact you, which Charlie never hesitated to remind me of whenever he saw me."

"Oh, God…was he rude? I mean I told him to gently hint to you that I didn't want to be contacted but…" she trailed off, not knowing how to finish. Charlie was overprotective and if he thought Remi was on the verge of finding her out and exposing her, he'd do whatever he could to prevent that.

"He was rude, but that's cool. I can respect him for wanting to protect you."

"Remi? I didn't expect to see you here," a voice said from behind them. "You weren't at the—" She swallowed the rest of her words when Camille and Remi turned around.

Sonya Brandt. She was the last person Camille wanted to see today.

"Oh… Camille. I didn't see you there. I heard you were in town. I guess a third trip to the hospital *finally* got you to come see your dad," she said snidely. "How lucky are we to have you back." That last sentence came out strained as if it hurt the woman to say it.

She didn't have to fake with Camille because Camille was completely aware that Sonya Brandt did not care for her. The feeling was mutual, with good reason. The woman had tried to come between Camille and Remi on several occasions and those were just the times she knew about. Sonya was a viper in designer stilettos. Camille still wasn't sure how she got a law degree, since she remembered Sonya not caring about school very much. Maybe her parents threatened to cut her off if she didn't get herself together. But maybe she was a good lawyer. She had to be if she was the lawyer for Krane Foods…unless there was something else going on there. But she'd asked and Remi had answered and she believed he wasn't ever involved with Sonya. Not that it mattered, because once she made sure her father was well enough to take care of himself properly, she'd be going back to New York and her life.

But if returning to New York was a good idea, why wasn't she more excited about going back to the place she called home? Why was she getting uneasy about Sonya Brandt's presence in Remi's everyday life?

She gave Sonya the once-over. "Sonya, you haven't changed one bit." The statement was meant to be a compliment wrapped in an insult. Her scowl, her dirty looks, her superior attitude were all still the same, but Camille could admit that the woman looked like a million bucks. She was tall and lean, with hair down her back. She had flawless skin, perfect teeth, and flirty eyes. Hell, if she weren't straight, she'd go after the girl herself.

Camille could easily see why Sonya's presence would be threatening, but Camille did well to hide her insecurities. When they were younger she'd never nagged Remi about what he was doing and whom he was doing it with. Her theory had always been that if he cheated on her then he wasn't hers to begin with, so good riddance. Yeah, she would've had a broken heart if they'd broken up, but nagging someone about cheating wasn't the type of thing Camille did. And anyway, she'd ended up causing her own broken heart when she'd left.

Sonya smiled. "I know, right? Good genes, probably. I should give you the card for my personal trainer. He could really help." She then scrunched her nose and looked up as if she was thinking of all the ways her personal trainer could help Camille. Camille simply rolled her eyes and ignored her offer. She knew it was just a dig at her naturally curvy body. She was by no means large, but she had full breasts, a small waist, a high, curvy rear end, and what Southern folks called childbearing hips. No, she did not fit a model's size at a few inches over five feet and a size eight, but she liked her curves. Sonya's observations were irrelevant.

Remi cleared his throat, taking the focus away from the growing tension between the women. "What brings you downtown, Sonya?"

"Oh, you know…getting some lunch and support-
ing our booth. You know the one we planned together
in your office that night. We should do it again." She
then walked off, her heels clicking a few times before
she stopped and turned around to Remi. "Oh…Santos
told me to thank you for the graduation gift to Vegas for
him and his friends. He's having the time of his life,"
Sonya said, mentioning her younger brother."

"No problem. He's a smart kid and there is nothing shabby about graduating second in your class. He
earned the trip."

Sonya then smiled. There was something personal
there and Camille did not like it at all. She was jealous.
It was an annoying emotion but there it was… Sonya
and Remi had been intimate and Sonya didn't mind
letting her know. But what had Camille confused was
her suggestion that she and Remi had slept together recently. Camille decided to ignore the woman because
she was probably trying to get under her skin, a mission she had accomplished.

Camille had no idea what was going on with her.
She'd remained oblivious to the menial stressors of life
by not dating anyone seriously and mostly focusing on
her career. Her only real friends were her agent and
Charlie, and the only events she went to were those
Anna forced her to attend. So these newfound emotions
were confusing her. Her feelings about the way Sonya
looked at Remi, Remi's declarations of love, people in
the town shunning her, and the possibility of someone
putting the pieces together and finding out that she was
Reese Elaine…it was all talking a toll on her. It was

this town. She'd been here much too long already. That much was obvious.

That was it. She needed to leave this place. It didn't matter that she loved Remi. She had yet to say it out loud so she could cut her losses and hope one day she'd find someone who'd help her forget about Remington Krane. Or maybe her career would be her happiness and it would be enough to fulfill her.

The smirk Sonya gave Camille before finally sauntering off said it all. She was issuing a challenge. She did not like the fact that Camille was back in town and it was even worse that she was with Remi. Sonya had had him to herself all these years and Camille's presence was derailing any progress she'd made with Remi. That made Camille just the slightest bit satisfied with herself, but it also made her wary of Sonya. Just what did the woman have up her sleeve and how long would it be before she made her move—whatever that may be?

Chapter 11

"Okay… I promise this outing is going to get better. Sonya was just being Sonya, you know that."

Camille nodded in understanding and Remington was relieved. He'd been with women who would've made a big deal out of what Sonya had implied. He had to remember that Camille was unlike any other woman he'd known. She wasn't up for the drama or games. She didn't let the Sonyas of the world get to her and if she did, she did an excellent job of covering up her feelings.

"It's fine," she said. "Let's eat. There better be some of my favorite snack left when we get to your booth. I want my favorite dessert."

And that's what they did. He took her mind off nosey people by flirting and keeping her attention on the next booth. There were a few people who recognized her, but thankfully they were all very nice. If they felt negatively about her being in town, they didn't show it. For the next hour they ate and laughed and he was amazed at the amount of food such a little body could put away.

After about the fourth booth, Camille declared that she was stuffed but wasn't leaving until she got her favorite snack to take back with her.

"I sent you enough to last for a couple months or more," he told her.

She laughed and waggled her brows. "I can never have enough."

That one simple statement flared Remi's desire and he kissed her passionately right in the middle of downtown Fairdell in front of the people who'd be voting for him in a little over a year's time. If they'd gotten away with avoiding attention before, that was no longer the case because all eyes were now tracking the amorous couple.

Before Camille had a chance to be embarrassed Remi grabbed her by the hand and dragged her over to the Krane Gourmet Snack Foods booth. There were several interns there as well as David, the Employee Communications and Morale Specialist for the company.

"David, how are things going? Lot of people stopping by?"

"Of course. And who do we have here?" David said, ignoring business to find out who Camille was. "I don't think I've seen this beauty around town." His intent look had Camille's cheeks flaming.

"This is Camille Ryan, she is—"

"Reese's daughter…oh, yeah… He speaks highly of

you. But I thought you'd be wearing a habit and singing hymns. He always made you sound like a saint. He never said you were an angel."

Remi chuckled at David. The man was laying it on thick. He even kissed her hand when she offered to shake his. He was a charmer in every way and usually got the girl even with the lame one-liners. But not this time. Camille was his.

Blond-haired, blue-eyed David Wunner had a frat-boy persona and often flippant ways, but he was exactly who Remi needed to run into that night at the bar. Their personal and professional views were similar, which led to a great conversation and a friendship that had lasted six years.

Remi had been at an Atlanta bar nursing a drink after he'd been told by his grandfather that he would be in charge of Krane Foods. Frederick's health had deteriorated to a point where he could no longer deal with the day-to-day responsibilities of running the company and he had decided to hand over the reins to him. Remi had been basically running the company anyway since he was twenty-one, but at twenty-four—a little over a year after he was done with graduate school, being named CEO had been a lot to take in. He'd known he could make the company even more successful but the weight of the position had driven him to drink.

David had been in a similar way that night after having lost his job as head of human resources for a top shipping company. They'd started talking and David had told him of his idea to take human resources to another level by having employee team-building activities like company picnics, holiday parties and family days as well as volunteering opportunities and community outreach—all sponsored by the company.

Remi had been surprised that the company David worked for had fired him. He didn't understand how a company would not want to implement such ideas. If employees were happy and fulfilled, then productivity would increase. It was a win-win. He knew that was what Krane needed under his guidance. He came up with a position right there on the spot and the next week David had started working for him.

Camille cleared her throat, bringing Remi out of his memories. "Uh, thanks," she said. "I know my father brags…but I'm no saint or angel."

Remi protested. "She's all that and more. Don't let her fool you, Dave. She's just being modest."

"Sounds like you know something about Ms. Ryan. I hope that's not the case because then I'd be poaching my best friend's woman."

Camille laughed at David's antics. "Oh, I need to watch out for you. You're a bad one." David winked at her and then gave Remi a look that said that Remi had some explaining to do about Camille. Remi knew his friend had never seen him holding hands with any woman since they'd known each other. Remi was the type who avoided getting serious, not wanting to get close to anyone for fear of losing them the way he'd lost Camille. But if he were being honest, he'd admit his heart belonged to Camille and he would've never given it away to anyone else.

David smiled a sly smile. "Bad enough to have the

teacher punish me?" he asked Camille. "That's always been a fantasy of mine."

"How did you know I was...?"

"Your dad, remember? We worked together on a beautification project at the Krane Foods headquarters. He helped me figure out a way to get the employees involved. He couldn't stop talking about his 'Bug.'"

"Oh, God..." Camille put her hand to her face in embarrassment. Remi loved the adorable groan she emitted. It sounded just like her groan that morning, when he'd first entered her. It had been followed by a soft mewl and then a purr and... *He wanted her again.*

"Ahem." David chuckled and looked at Remi knowingly. "Why don't you take the old man home? He looks tired." David reached into his shirt pocket and pulled out a card. "Take this for when you're ready for a little vanilla in your coffee."

Remi mouthed a thanks to David as he plucked the card from her fingers. His friend was a flirt but Remi was sure his friend was aware that Camille was different. The look on Remi's face probably said it all. He was sure he had some explaining to do at the office in the morning.

"See you at the office tomorrow."

Remi and Camille moved away from David and over to the front of the booth. He took the time to speak to the interns before he and Camille made their way back around the square to where his car was parked.

He shook his head and chuckled at himself because he'd been so caught up in showing her off they'd forgotten to get her snacks. Hopefully he would keep her so distracted that she wouldn't notice.

Remi had thoroughly enjoyed their afternoon, but now he wanted her alone. He'd been torturing himself with fleeting touches and that explosive kiss in the middle of the square. She'd been smiling and flirting and making it known that she wanted him, too. He hadn't missed her jealousy while talking to Sonya, and it had turned him on to know that Camille had possessive thoughts toward him. It gave him hope that he may have a chance at convincing her she needed to be back in Fairdell with him to stay.

Remington opened the car door for Camille, but he couldn't wait any longer to kiss her again. "Wait. Don't get in yet."

She gave him a confused look over her shoulder but complied. She then turned and waited for whatever it was he wanted.

Camille waited for Remi to give her a reason for the holdup. She stood there hoping that he was about to touch her. She'd been longing for it since they'd left his bed—or the ottoman, she corrected herself—but she didn't want to think about what that meant for her. She knew she was riding a thin line when it came to her warring feelings. And it didn't help when Remi looked at her and made her want to feel that amorous gaze on her every day.

That thought led her to a bigger worry—she had some decisions to make. She had to figure out how to reveal her career to her father and others, and also how to make up all those years to Remi. He probably wouldn't want her to think about him in terms of a debt, but she couldn't help it. She owed him for leaving and she'd find a way to make it up to him regardless of whether or not she stayed in town.

Had she really just considered staying in town? Yes, she had. If it meant being near Remi, maybe she could give it a try. It would certainly make Anna happy if she decided to reveal her true identity to her readers. That would mean Anna would get to book Camille on signings and other public events that would help boost her into superstardom, not that Camille wanted that.

What she did want was Remi. She could admit that to herself. If he was willing to forgive her, then she needed to start forgiving herself...for everything. She'd spent her entire life blaming herself for issues that were out of her control, like her mother's death. She needed to forgive herself, and one way to start was to come clean to her father about her feelings so she could let go of some of her guilt.

"I want to kiss you, but I don't want to stop there, Camille," Remi whispered, his lips close to her ear. A moment ago, she'd felt the same, but her wayward thoughts were like a bucket of ice extinguishing her desire, bringing her back to reality.

"I... I... Remi, I feel so guilty about my mother." That was not what she'd intended to say, but it was what had come out. It was her thoughts taking on a life of their own and her guilt manifesting itself. She started to sob and though she had not spoken a word about this previously, he seemed to understand and pushed his desire aside to offer Camille the comfort she needed.

Remi pulled her head to his chest and let her cry. She apologized to him for ruining his expensive shirt as she cried. He chuckled. "You're a bestselling author and you're worried about a shirt that we both can afford a million times over. God, you're like a breath of fresh air, Ladybug. I know you're hurting but I have to say this... We'll go back to my place and talk, but when you're all better, I plan to make sure Reese Elaine has plenty of ideas for her next book."

She sniffled and smiled through her hurt. He put her in the car then and closed the door. She cried a little, but felt better that Remi wouldn't allow her to bury herself in irrational guilt. His proposition to talk and then make her forget about her troubles was one she definitely wouldn't pass on. They needed to talk. She needed to confess and purge. Then and only then would she be ready to think about a future for them.

A future for them. The thought made her stomach flutter in anticipation, letting Camille know she was making the right choice.

"I think I'm going to tell my dad about my writing," she blurted once she'd removed her shoes and sweater and made herself comfortable in Remi's home. "It's time he knows. He needs to be able to make his own decisions regarding my career and he can't if he doesn't know what I do for a living. I want him to be proud of me, Remi." She wiped away a tear. "I'm sorry, I don't mean to be so weepy."

"Nonsense. We came here to talk and that's what we're doing. I'm glad that you feel comfortable enough to trust me with your feelings," Remi confessed and pulled her up from where she was sitting and into his waiting arms. "Your father won't care if you're a teacher or not. He's always been proud of you."

"Please remind me to give you back that gift card." Camille suddenly remembered when Remi mentioned being a teacher. "You should probably find someone who is actually a teacher to give it to or maybe you could donate it to the local elementary school."

He didn't speak for a moment. "I have a confession to make… I've been sending anonymous donations to your school—well, the school I thought you taught at. I also know your grocer, Mr. Donati. I made sure he had your favorite snack in his store." He then told her how he found out where she lived in New York, contacted Mr. Donati and made sure his shelves were always stocked.

"That was really sweet of you," Camille admitted. She swung on a covered porch swing that offered a great view of Remi's sprawling backyard. She looked at him beside her. "I think I'm done crying now." She then laughed at herself. She had not been this much of a mess since leaving Remi in Fairdell ten years ago.

"Good, because I don't like it when you cry. But if you do want to, I'm here." Remi draped his arm around her and pulled her close. He kissed the top of her head in a gesture of support. "So, we're going to tell your father? When?"

"*We?* Rem, you don't have to do that. This is my prob—"

"I'm not allowing you to brush me off. I want to be present for every important event in your life," Remi said and she knew he meant it by the way he looked at her. "I want to show you that regardless of time and distance, I never stopped loving you."

His comforting words were laced with remnants of pain. She'd caused that pain. Looking down at his hand she realized she'd wanted to hear those words from him for the past ten years. She'd not seriously dated because subconsciously she was waiting for this moment. The moment where she returned to him and he forgave her, the moment where he released her from her guilt, and told her that he'd never stopped loving her. She could write from anywhere. But Remi was here and he had a billion-dollar company to run. If she wanted him, she had to choose Fairdell over New York. She had to choose Remi over New York. She had to choose what she wanted over anything else.

"I..." Camille placed her hand over Remi's. The three words were right there on the tip of her tongue but she couldn't seem to get them to come out.

"I love you enough for both of us, Camille," Remi avowed and placed a palm against the side of her cheek. She leaned into that warm hand and felt relief that Remi could sense her feelings but was patient enough to wait to hear her say them. He was patient and forgiving and he loved her despite her choices and her faults.

So, why couldn't she say the words if she truly felt them?

Once those words were uttered, she could not take them back. It would be too late and she'd be devastated for putting herself out there. But Remi was worth the risk, wasn't he?

Definitely.

"Please kiss me, Rem. I want to show you..." She couldn't say the words, but she could show him how much she loved him and wanted to be with him. It was a big step for Camille to be a little selfish. She'd always been one to consider how her actions affected others, which was why she'd chosen to leave all those years ago. However, that time was over. She didn't want to be without him any longer. She wanted Remington Krane and she wasn't going to allow anything to keep them apart again—not her choices or his. From now on, they were together and they'd make decisions together.

Once again Camille felt that flutter in her belly that let her know she was making the right decision.

Chapter 12

Remi could see Camille was still afraid that he would change his mind and realize he hadn't forgiven her after all. She also feared that her father wouldn't support her career.

She had no reason to worry. Remington would be there for her if she let him. She wouldn't have to deal with any of the fallout from revealing that she was Reese Elaine, without him by her side.

So with his reassurance out of the way, he buried his hands in her soft hair and pulled her close. Their breaths mingled and mixed and he savored the way her breaths shortened and labored from just one touch. Her back reflexively arched, jutting out her full bosom. The hand she had on his leg glided up to his chest and gripped the front of his button-down white shirt. She seemed to be pushing him and pulling him at the same time, but he wasn't about to let this woman back away from him. She'd proclaimed she'd wanted to show Remington proof of her love and he'd help her do just that.

"I'm going to make love to you, Camille. Out here in the open. Right now."

She shivered and her mouth fell open at his declaration. The gasp that followed was swallowed whole as Remi's gaze focused on her soft lips and a hungry smile broke out across his face.

Her mouth tasted sweet. It was the best taste ever. It was so delicious that he never wanted to stop tasting her and touching her. She was pliant and her little moans made his already straining erection grow even more impatient.

Remington wanted to have her delirious and edgy with need just as he was, so he decided to ignore his own need for now. He wanted her to feel the heady intoxication that her mere presence had on him.

Boiling over with lust, Remington knew the only way he wouldn't catch fire and burn to a crisp was if this woman helped calm him by... *Oh, man!*

A hand cupping him through his jeans surprised and excited his already throbbing member. Camille's hands went to work on his belt soon after. When she couldn't get him free fast enough, he helped her. He rose from the swing and started to undo his belt, but Camille boldly took control again. "Let me," she said and went to work on his pants, freeing him from the confines of his jeans and boxer-briefs. "We're alone, right? No one will come out here?" she asked and he thought he'd release prematurely at the sound of her desperate, lustful tone.

He nodded and was about to pull her up to stand before him so he could claim her mouth again, but Camille had other ideas. Her hand went on the base of his steel-hard erection at the same time her lips covered its mushroomed head. The unexpected heat of her mouth and the softness of her lips made him almost come apart on the spot. Her inexperience was endearing and her craving to explore and do things she'd never done made him want her more.

Her warm, wet mouth slowly dragged along the sides of his length. Her lips and tongue left a sizzling trail in their path as her hand stroked him, producing a bead of pleasure that she licked right up.

The sight of Camille before him caused a primal urge to take over and before he realized what he was doing, he'd given up on slow and sensual. The way she teased his erection with her lips should be outlawed. Her natural talent overshadowed her inexperience.

Remi took her down to the grass, forgetting his state of dress. He got caught in his lowered pants and they fell in a tangle of arms and legs and articles of clothing. They laughed heartily but the laughter quickly turned to roaming hands, smashing mouths, pleasured moans and writhing bodies.

Addictive…that was what Camille was. He couldn't get enough. Her skin was so damn silky and her belly was smooth and taut. Her rear was supple and more than a handful—firm and round. She was short, but her long legs were able to wrap around his waist with no problem allowing him to plunge deep into her core, gliding through the heated moisture of her arousal.

There, in the grass, there was no fear of anything that might come their way, only love. Two people exploring each other in the most primitive way and she loved it. Camille had not felt this attraction to anyone but Remi and had a feeling that she never would again. He was the only one who could make her forget all her inhibitions and act on her carnal desires. She had never put her mouth on a man so intimately and had not wanted to do anything else upon laying eyes on Remington's beautiful, jutting erection. She'd acted on instinct and it had surprised her that she'd enjoyed the taste and feel of him in her mouth.

She had loved the way her control over him had made him react. He'd gotten overwhelmed and had roughly thrown her to the ground and passionately mounted her. He was aggressive and dominant the way he tore off her clothes and she loved every minute of it. Camille couldn't see herself being like this with anyone but him. He made her this way and it was only fair that he got to reap the benefits.

"Oh, Remi...ohhh," Camille shouted when they'd been going at it vigorously, her hips meeting every one of his thrusts. She didn't care that they were in his backyard, out on the open, in the soft grass.

He flipped them over and Remi's hand roamed her torso and fondled her aching breasts. They moved around her back and to her butt, cupping her and squeezing her and separating her rear cheeks so he could poke and probe even deeper into the slick walls of her sex.

"Please don't leave me, Camille," Remi begged when he sat up and they were face-to-face. "Please stay with me and be with me and marry me and have a family with me. I want that for us, Camille."

With each word, his thrusts became slower and deeper, more purposeful. They were pressed together breast to pecs, mouths only millimeters apart, breathing the same breaths.

Not knowing how to respond, but knowing how she *wanted* to respond, Camille decided that she would stop running from the man who could make her feel this way. She'd stop fearing what would happen if she decided to choose Remi and Fairdell. She'd stop hiding from her father and come clean to him and everyone else in order to have the life she wanted.

"I love you, Remington Krane, and I want all those things for us, as well. I want you and…" Camille could no longer speak. The emotion of the moment seemed to overtake them both. Tears leaked from the corners of Camille's eyes and she could see Remi trying to stop his own. The words must've been like a match to him because he moaned Camille's name between slow, deep thrusts. His body seized and every one of his hard muscles tightened around her. His thickness swelled and jerked against her pleasure spot and they shared in a deliciously blissful release. They held on to each other as their sensitized skin vibrated and tingled and she swore that after a minute or so he came again, filling her with his warm seed once more.

She giggled. "We were supposed to be talking, Rem. What happened?"

"You happened. I can't resist you and now I don't have to. You're mine...officially. Now we get to tell the world."

"I have to tell my father and my agent first."

"Anna, you won't believe this but I'm ready."

The sound of Anna's squeal could be heard across the room and she didn't even have the speaker phone on. Remi laughed at Camille's agent and mouthed *I told you so*. She'd been afraid of how Anna would respond after Camille had spent years trying to keep her true identity a secret. Anna was a skeptic at times, but apparently not about this. "Before you start planning all the appearances and contacting the masses I need you to know that I'm going to be leaving New York."

Camille cringed when the loud "WHAT?" blared through the line. "You're leaving me in this godforsaken city alone?"

"I thought you loved New York, Anna."

"Hell, no! I only say that because I am a modern woman with great fashion sense. I live on the Upper East Side and that is what people who live like me are supposed to say! I'd love to move to the suburbs to some small town and only go to the big city when I want to let loose a little." She sighed. "I can't believe you're leaving me."

But then Camille told her that real news. "I'm getting married, Anna. I'm staying here to be with my man." Camille liked saying that. She had a man. And it was the man she'd dreamed of being with all her life. She'd known Remi since she could remember and had had a crush on him before they ever started dating.

That statement launched Anna into a whole inquisition. Anna had known that there was only one man who could've swayed Camille so her friend didn't bother to ask who; she only wanted Camille to be sure about her choice. And when Camille assured her she'd returned to her one true love, Anna squealed again. She was happy and proud Camille had finally come to her senses in her love life and professional life. She and Anna weren't only business associates, they were friends, as well. They cared what happened to one another.

"I'm so happy for you, Camille," Anna finally said. "Now let me get off this phone so I can start planning. I feel like a mom planning her daughter's arrival into womanhood. This is going to be awesome. Expect me in town by the end of the week. I just said no to a really huge book signing and I have to call them back. I want to make your coming out a big deal, okay? So try to keep this under wraps for just a bit longer. We'll have an official unveiling soon so just keep this among your closest family and friends. Gotta to go, babe. Ciao!"

And that was that. The easy part. Now it was time for the hard part—talking to her father.

"I'm assuming she took the news well?" Remi had just walked back into his family room after he'd left to take a phone call. He carried an uneasy expression, almost as if he'd gotten bad news but was trying to cover it up by focusing on her.

"Is everything okay? You look like you just got some bad news."

"No… I mean yes… Everything is fine. Just some work stuff."

Camille believed the call wasn't as innocent as he made it seem, but she decided to drop it for now since she had a bounty of other stuff on her plate to contend with.

However, her mind wouldn't let it go, so she asked, "Rem, are you *really* sure about us? Can you—"

A finger to Camille's lips silenced her. "There is nothing to forgive," he said, anticipating her words. "I have every confidence you would have found your way back to me eventually. You aren't the malicious type, Ladybug." He made her stand and face him. As his hands settled on her hips and their bodies aligned Camille's skin prickled through the thin T-shirt he'd given her after ripping off her dress. "You went to a city where you were able to realize your dream. I'd never want to take that away from you, so maybe life was meant to unfold this way."

"*This* was meant to be, Rem. My dad being sick may have brought me here, but you're why I'm staying. I hope you're ready to deal with my lifestyle because there will be travel, there will be fans and there will be—"

"Me and you. Nothing else matters. And I'd be happy to be your trophy husband," he joked. "I plan to be by your side at every event I possibly can. You know your fans want to see what true inspiration looks like."

He then flexed his muscles and a slight shiver moved through her as she giggled.

Camille played off the shiver as fake and rolled her eyes. She then slapped Remi playfully on the chest. "You are too much. But maybe you should stay away from my work. I don't want to be on some daytime gossip show for getting into a fistfight at a book signing because some groupie thinks you're one of the heroes from my books."

"Think I'm that good-looking, do you?" he asked arrogantly and then placed a kiss on Camille's lips and held her closer. "Maybe I should be the model on your next book cover. We can make this a partnership."

"Yes, I do think you're that good-looking, but you should probably keep your day job. I don't share well." Camille stepped away from Remi because it was getting hot. Her uncontrollable need for Remi was ridiculous and they needed to separate before they were at it again. She needed to talk to her father and she wanted to do it before she lost her nerve. But damn if she could make her legs move with Remi's face buried in her neck and his hands on her butt and his...

Maybe they had a little time to spare.

Chapter 13

Once exploring fingers dipped into her wetness, Camille had been a goner. Over and over again Remington had brought her to her release until she was no longer able to move a limb. She'd fallen asleep in his arms before they'd even had a chance to disconnect their sweat-slicked bodies.

And now he was doing what a man who was whipped beyond description usually did the morning after the woman he loved made him scream like a girl.

He was making breakfast.

He placed food on a tray with her favorite dessert. He then added a cup of orange juice and coffee as well, before he deposited a black velvet box among the items.

The ring was his grandmother's. Frederick Krane had given it to his woman years ago. Now Remi's grandmother rested in heaven and he hoped she was looking down on him in approval, knowing he was giving her ring to someone he loved and wanted to be with, and not out of obligation or circumstance.

Walking into the room, he licked his lips at the glorious sight of Camille's half-uncovered body. She was lying on her belly with her arms under the pillow and her head on top. Her skin glowed from a combination of the sun's morning rays and the contrast of her bronze skin against the stark white sheets. The swell of her buttocks peeked out from under the sheet, leaving him to imagine the feel of the mounds of flesh in his hands and mouth.

He set the tray down, unable to resist reaching for her. He had to wake her up so she could eat and so he could propose properly.

He had to touch her, right?

That would be his excuse.

But the truth of the matter was he needed her more than he needed anything else, and touching her was the only way he could even begin to satisfy that need.

Remington's hands found a path under the sheet and over the curve of her rear as he leaned into her sleeping form. He grazed her shoulder with his stubble. She squirmed and then sighed before turning over. She dazzled him with a smile and her hands instinctively went to the back of his freshly shaven head to pull him close for a kiss. An ardent morning greeting with a little dry-humping thrown in.

"I made you breakfast, Ladybug. You hungry?"

"For you? Definitely."

"As much as I'd like to take you up on your offer," he said removing her hand from inside his cotton pajama pants, "I think you may want what's on this tray more than you want—"

"Never. I could never want anything more than I want you. I know that now, Rem." Of course, her words were about more than just breakfast. She was speaking of her career. She was willing to deal with staying in a town where people may judge her for her writing in order to be with him. She was willing to face her father's potential disappointment so she didn't have to hide who she was any longer. She was willing to leave the life she'd come to know over the past ten years so they could be together.

She was willing to do all of these things for him and he still wasn't being honest with her. And the call he'd received yesterday reminded Remington of that fact. His petition to run for mayor had been approved and soon it would be public knowledge. Some knew of his intent, but it wasn't official until that document became public record.

Remi cursed himself several times as he thought about Camille's potential reaction to the news of his campaign. He was sure she'd try to sacrifice their personal happiness once again so he could have the best chance at happiness in his career. He couldn't allow her to protect him again.

Remington could admit he'd let a lot of things get away from him since Camille's reappearance into his life. He'd usually be at the office until late at night and return early in the morning. He'd been singularly focused and it had resulted in success. Then had come the day he'd filled out that petition and received the last signature needed to enter the election and he'd considered that day to be a success. And while Remington had thought those successes had brought him the happiness he needed, he realized he wasn't truly fulfilled until Camille walked back into his life. He realized he wanted more. He realized he'd been missing something and he hadn't even known it.

Maybe he should just tell Camille and let her decide what to do with the information about his political aspirations. It was too late for her to take back her proclamations of love and trust in their relationship. Surely she'd see that they were adults and that there was no reason for them to make the hard sacrifices anymore. She'd make a perfect first lady for him and the people of Fairdell. She cared about people, she wanted the best for them no matter what opinion they held of her. She'd kept a pseudonym to not only protect her father and Remi, but to protect their religious little town from possible negative attention. He could imagine the kind of press the town would get if the media found out who Camille was and where she was from. They'd make a big deal out of the fact that such a prominent voice in erotic fiction came from a town like Fairdell.

But she was willing to put herself out there because of him and he couldn't allow her to regret her decision by thinking he was a liar. However, he'd have to approach the subject delicately. Maybe he could contact Charlie and her father and ask for their help in making her understand why he had chosen to keep it from her until now. He'd do anything to stop her from feeling as if she had to run again in order to protect him.

Remi kissed her forehead one more time before pulling away from Camille so he could propose the right way. But her body was too much of a distraction and the fact that she was naked and he could smell her arousal in the air was… *Oh, forget this!*

She had him when she licked her lips and let the sheet drop from where he'd tucked it under her arms. Her exposed nipples were hard. They were taunting him. Remi leaned in and took one taut nipple into his mouth and Camille moaned, her legs falling wide for him in invitation. Her hands reached out for the waistband of his pajama pants but he was strong and stopped her before things got too out of hand. He stood quickly and backed away from her, needing the distance.

"I didn't come in here for this…not that I don't want to," Remi said very seriously. When she started to giggle he wondered what was so funny about his frustration. But when he looked at where her gaze had landed, he saw that his length tented his pajama pants and there was no way he could be taken seriously now.

He shared in her laugh at his expense. He then shocked her by stripping out of his clothes and diving onto the bed. "I'm only giving in because you won't take me seriously in my…condition."

"Oh, I take you very seriously in this condition. And I don't mind helping with the cure for your particular ailment," Camille flirted and for the next hour the pair cured Remi's condition.

* * *

"Okay, now I need food. Bacon, please."

Remi had just opened his eyes after their lovemaking put them both to sleep for a short nap. Camille lay there facing him, awaiting his response. He didn't speak, instead reached one long arm over to the tray she'd forgotten was there and placed a piece of cold bacon in front of her face. She didn't take it from him, but let him feed her until they'd gone through three pieces this way without speaking.

Camille thought he was reaching for a fourth piece, but he instead presented her with a little black velvet box. A ring box.

She sat bolt upright when he set the box down between them and opened it. Before she could blink he was off the bed and on his knee with the ring in his hand.

"Remi? What do you think you're doing and where did you get—"

Of course she knew what he was doing because they'd talked about it already. They'd agreed that they wanted the same things from their relationship. But she'd thought it would be some time in the future before they took this step. She'd thought they would maybe date and get to know each other and make up for lost time. She didn't consider that he would be putting a ring on her finger so soon.

"This ring belonged to my grandmother and then my mother. It was at the jeweller's when she died in the accident, and I've been able to treasure it all these years. They were both given this ring on their first anniversary and it was meant to be passed down to my wife on our first anniversary. I've been apart from you for too long and I can't wait until our first anniversary. I told myself that I would give this ring to you on the day you told me you loved me again. And even though that day was yesterday, I hope—"

"Yes!" Camille laughed and put her hand out to him, wiggling her fingers playfully. It was unlike the reaction she would've expected from herself. She never thought she'd be this excited. But deep down she'd always wanted this for herself.

"I have yet to ask anything so you need to sit your sexy butt down and wait for me to finish," he teased. "Now, where was I? Oh, yeah…I hope and pray that I can make up for the hurt you endured when you made that decision for us. I hope you'll let me show you how much I love you for the rest of our lives. I want you to accept this ring and promise that I will do whatever it takes to make you happy. Will you be my wife, Camille Elise Ryan?" he asked and stared at her, waiting for her answer.

She sat quietly, making sure he was finished with his speech. She then threw her arms around him and tackled him with her naked body. She screamed yes over and over until the reason for her screams wasn't an engagement ring.

Camille was going through clothes quickly and it wasn't as if she could just wash them and wear them again. Remi had destroyed her favorite casual dress the other night. But he was ever the thoughtful man because when he'd left her to soak her aching limbs in his bathtub, he'd tried to make it up to her by getting her clothes from her father's house since she was too embarrassed to do it herself.

She couldn't believe he'd done something so thoughtful. But as she stood there looking at the clothes he held out to her, it hit her.

"Oh, my God, Rem. What did Daddy say when you showed up to pick up my clothes?" She was still innocent in her father's eyes and she wanted to remain that way—at least a little longer.

However, Remington remained tight-lipped about his conversation with her father. He only said he had everything under control and Camille believed him.

"I've already picked out something for you to wear," he proclaimed, changing the subject. Camille could tell he was proud of himself for completing the task. She raised an eyebrow at him, but he shocked her when he handed her a pair of designer jeans, a flowy green camisole with a white exposed zipper detail on the back, and a white cropped blazer with rolled sleeves. There was also a pair of nude pumps and a clutch to match. The G-string and strapless bra were nude as well and Camille glared at him for providing her with such skimpy underwear for a simple dinner with her father.

Remi threw his hands up in surrender. "What? They are all yours, right? I just chose from what you had."

The both chuckled and Camille left to get dressed.

Chapter 14

"I am so glad you could make it," Bernice Savage gushed and Remi could feel Camille tense at his side. She'd complained that she would rather stay at his house in bed than go to a dinner with the woman who seemed hell-bent on making her uncomfortable around her own father. He wasn't exactly sure what Bernice's deal was but she seemed to show an unnecessary amount of hostility toward Camille, as if she was personally offended by Camille's existence.

Maybe tonight they'd find out the cause of her hostility or maybe she was just jealous. Reese Ryan cared a great deal about his daughter and he wasn't shy about singing her praises to anyone who would listen. The man was so blindly proud that he never noticed the disparaging looks people gave him when he spoke fondly of his daughter. Most still saw Camille as the girl who'd broken the heart of the city's most influential resident's grandson. They saw her having threatened their perfect little town in some way. And they resented her for leaving and not coming back as many other Fairdell natives had. Charlie, Sonya, Remi and a whole host of other Fairdell natives had returned to contribute to the success of the town; however, Camille was one of the rare ones who had not.

What people didn't know was *why* she hadn't. If people knew she'd sacrificed a future with him so he could have a future at Krane Foods and be a leader in the city he loved, they wouldn't be so quick to judge her. But they'd never know the real reason and he only hoped she could deal with the potential hostility, especially when they found out what she did for a living.

He had to show people that he loved her regardless of her leaving and regardless of what she did for a living. He needed to be the example. Some people would fall in line and follow his lead because they respected him, but others...they'd swear that Camille was some Jezebel who hurt men for fun, especially when they found out about Reese Elaine.

They were so wrong about his fiancée. He'd defend her. He'd protect her. He'd show her that it didn't matter what anyone else thought about her being his wife and first lady. His love would erase all the negativity and hatred.

"I'm so glad you invited me, Ms. Savage. But I think I'd follow Camille anywhere," Remi said and kissed

Camille on the top of the head. He could feel her relax beside him a little.

"I told you to call me Bernice," the older woman fussed and placed a hand on Remi's arm, smiling the whole time. "Oh, Camille…I wasn't even paying attention to you standing there. Not used to you being around here, I guess." It was a dig at Camille. Remington didn't like it but he chose to hold his tongue. He wasn't one to disrespect an elder. He'd been brought up better than that.

"Where is Daddy? Why are you answering the door?" Camille snapped, and Remi had never seen her behave this way. It was like a mama cub protecting the baby cub, except in this case the baby cub was her father and the mama was a protective daughter who didn't trust the intentions of the woman standing before her.

"He had to go…get cleaned up. That man…" Ms. Savage got a look on her face that made Remi uncomfortable. It was obvious the woman was talking about some sexual encounter they'd had before he and Camille arrived and she absolutely wanted Camille to know what had taken place, especially when she finished her thought. Remington shook his head at how the older crowd felt they could say anything and get away with it as Bernice said, "That man is very *fit* for his age. Probably where you learned—"

"Bernice, I think I smell something burning," a voice said from behind Bernice, cutting off the insult that was about to fly from her lips. Remi was grateful even though the save had come from Charlie. Camille's hands had started to sweat and she seemed to be stifling the urge to punch the loose-lipped older woman in the face. He probably would've enjoyed seeing it since Bernice deserved it, but he couldn't allow Camille to do something she'd regret.

Bernice scurried off and Charlie emerged. His gaze went straight down to their joined hands, where Remi played with the large diamond absently. Thankfully Bernice had not noticed, giving them time to make the announcement, but Charlie wasn't so oblivious and zeroed in on the stunning piece of jewelry.

"So are congratulations in order?"

Remington was surprised by how friendly the question sounded. And what surprised him even more was the approving nod he received from Camille's best friend. He guessed the man had had time to think about Remington's visit and realized all Remington wanted was for Camille to be happy. If the look on her face was anything to go by, she was more than happy. His already full heart swelled even more knowing he was the one who'd made her so ecstatic.

Camille beamed at her friend and waved the fingers of her left hand playfully. Remington chuckled and said to Charlie, "I love her and I'll never hurt her." Charlie nodded that he understood and Remington continued. "Over the next few months Camille will need you *and* me and Reese. She is moving back to town and she is coming out as Reese Elaine."

Camille smiled up at Remi. The grateful look in her eyes wasn't something he could ignore. He was compelled to make love to her right then and there but restrained himself from doing anything more than pressing a lingering kiss to her soft, full lips.

Charlie grabbed Camille and pulled her into a bear hug. Her feet came off the floor and she giggled. "So my partner in crime is returning to stir up some trouble with me?" Charleston joked, but there was nothing but affection in his eyes when he asked the question. Camille nodded, and Charleston hugged her tighter. "I always knew you wanted to return, but I also knew why you wanted to stay away so I accepted your decision." Looking over at Remi he added, "I should've known he would be the one that would be able to get you to come back."

The hug lingered a bit too long for Remi's tastes and he jokingly commented, "Okay, okay, unhand my fiancée."

"Fiancée? Who's getting married?" Reese Ryan asked as he came down the steps with a huge smile on his face. It was the smile of a man who'd been thoroughly satisfied. Remi didn't know whether to be slightly disgusted, concerned for the man's heart, or smile that the man still had it like that. He'd known some of the other single women in town had gone after Reese and he'd heard that some of them were at odds with one another over his affections. Reese didn't seem to take any of them seriously. Camille had once told him that her father said he'd never marry again because there was only one woman he'd ever had eyes for and that was her mother, Elaine Ryan. Camille had been sad after revealing that, and Remi knew it was because she felt it was her fault that her father could no longer have happiness with Elaine.

Smiling at Reese's attempt at ignorance, Remington recalled the conversation he'd had with the man earlier that day. When he'd come to pick up Camille's clothing, he'd also talked to her father about proposing to Camille. Remington had already done so and Camille had said yes by that time, but out of respect he'd asked her dad anyway.

He'd let Reese know he had every intention of making an honest woman out of Camille. He'd also confessed his plans to run for mayor and his fear that Camille would run away to protect him again. At first he'd expected the older man to tell him to allow Camille to make her own decisions and not force her to give up the career she'd established, but Reese hadn't done that. Reese Ryan had got choked up and said he couldn't think of anything that would make him happier than to have his Bug close by. His approval had proved emotional and Remington had had to leave for fear both men would regret the unguarded display of sentiment.

"Well, I guess it's no longer a secret," Camille said and pranced over to her father holding her hand behind her back. She then flashed her hand at him and Remi took his place next to her. Remi heard Charlie leave and head toward the kitchen to give them privacy.

"You're finally making an honest woman of my baby, Remington?" the older man said and winked at him over Camille's head.

"Yes, sir. I love your daughter, Reese."

The older man nodded and then returned his gaze to his daughter. "This what you want, Bug?"

"Yes, Daddy. I—"

"My baby is moving back? Hallelujah! You are all right with me, Remington Krane," Reese bellowed and then clapped Remi on the shoulder, cutting his daughter off. "You two have made this old man's night. I can't begin to describe how happy I am," Reese said as he hugged Camille tightly.

Reese then joined Bernice and Charlie in the kitchen, leaving the newly engaged couple alone.

"Are you happy?" Remi asked Camille. She nodded right before she stepped into his arms.

Camille's eyes were full of love and appreciation, letting him know they were taking the right next step. Remi loved it when Camille looked at him that way. There in her eyes, it was clear as crystal that she loved him. It wasn't new love either. It was love revived or love never lost. Love returned. She'd loved him all these years and it was evident in her gaze, in her touch, in the tone of her voice when she spoke to him. It was enough to turn him into a sentimental fool *and* turn him on at the same time.

Remi's mouth descended upon Camille's and without hesitation his tongue invaded her mouth. Her hands moved up his chest and around his neck. His own hands lowered to her waist and then her rear, nearly lifting her off the floor.

Remi's lips stroked and caressed, mimicking the way he'd made love to her earlier that day. He reveled in her taste and feel as their passion grew. Remi knew that they should stop. They were not in a place where they could finish what they were starting, but neither of them seemed to care in that moment. Things were going well, and taking time to enjoy one another was something he was glad to do at any time and in any place. This was his woman and he wanted the world to know he had such a beautiful, intelligent, talented woman on his arm and in his life forever.

Not even realizing he'd done it, he'd backed Camille into the wall next to the staircase. "I want you so bad, Camille."

"I know. I want you, too. How'd you like to see my room again after all these years?"

Camille didn't have to ask him twice and he led the way up the stairs. He knew exactly where he was going. His purposeful stride made her have to stifle a laugh so no one would hear them escaping. She and Remi were not being discreet and she was sure someone would come looking for them soon.

He opened the door to her room and stopped briefly. He seemed to be taking in the room that looked the same as it had ten years ago. There was still high school memorabilia, old pictures and quotes on the wall she'd painted on freehand. The moment came and went quickly and before she knew it, Remington had her pinned against the door. His hands roamed her body and found the button of her jeans. Her hands dipped under the hem of his black button-down and felt the heated skin there. She moaned in delight when Remi's hand covered her mound with one hand as he pushed her jeans down with the other.

It was a frenzy of hands and fingers and lips and tongues and chucking aside of garments that only slowed when Remi had her legs free and his erection waiting. He entered her in one smooth thrust and he covered her mouth to silence the moan he knew would come with his delicious invasion into her core.

Camille's legs were wrapped around his waist and she held on to him. Remi plundered her and made her feel like this quick romp was just as drawn out as their previous relations.

The sex was hurried yet thorough. His upward motion was rough yet oh so refined and smooth. His words of love were enough to make her come and they did.

Burying her face in his neck to muffle her scream, her legs locked and the walls of her core clenched around him so tightly she thought she might be causing him pain. Obviously she wasn't hurting him because he surged into her with precise movements that had him following her over the edge. He wasn't able to control the volume of his growl during his release and called out her name as he held on to her for dear life.

They both came down from their release, panting heavily and chuckling at their lack of control.

After a minute of catching their collective breaths, Camille ordered Remi to leave so she could clean up. He said he'd text her from downstairs after he gauged whether or not the rest of the house had heard them. Thankfully a few minutes later she got a text saying no one seemed to notice they were missing as they were still setting the table and preparing food. Camille breathed a sigh of relief, but when she emerged from the room several minutes later she was surprised to see Charlie standing there, leaning against the wall of the hallway.

"Why are you standing here in the dark?" Camille asked before he could say anything.

"Just wanted to warn you that Ms. Savage isn't going to be playing fair. That woman…" Charlie shook his head. "Just don't let her make you upset. Don't worry about that whoring old battle-ax, and I won't let her get away with her little comments. Oh, and maybe we should sit down and have the birds and bees talk later," Charlie said as he chuckled.

He'd heard them. Camille should be embarrassed but she wasn't. Instead she playfully slapped him on the arm.

"Thank you for being happy for me, Charlie."

"I couldn't be anything else, babe."

Charlie had been right to warn her so she could prepare. He and Remi had to come to her rescue a few times during the evening. Ms. Savage had all but called her a whore, and her father, bless his sweet heart, was completely unaware of the woman's slights. The man was too decent for his own good because he saw the good in most people.

By the end of the night Ms. Savage had asked Remi for the tenth time if he was sure about getting married. Remi must've had enough because before dessert even arrived, he was whispering that he was ready to leave.

They left not long after, but not before Remi had encouraged Camille to pack whatever was left of her things to take over to his house. She quickly did that and they returned to his home.

Despite their mental tiredness, their desire for one another only elevated once they were alone. They barely made it through the door before clothes were ripped off and their bodies became entangled so they could pick up where they'd left off earlier that evening in her room.

Only making it to the stairs, they made love. Camille ignored the painful stab of the lightly carpeted stairs in her back. After her first release she declared that while she liked the spontaneity of being taken on the stairs, it was much too painful to continue. Remington solved that problem when he scooped her up and took her on the cold, hardwood floor, which was more comfortable than she'd expected it to be. Or maybe she was just so crazed for him that she hadn't paid attention to where she was at, only what she was doing and whom she was doing it with and the sheer state of ultimate bliss he took her to with each loving caress.

Chapter 15

"You can't stay at home again. Someone will tell your grandfather and that'll just give him another reason to hate me. I won't have him thinking I am taking you away from Krane Foods."

Camille and Remi had showered and eaten breakfast together. They'd been able to control themselves throughout much of the night and he woke feeling refreshed and happier than he'd been in a long time. The woman he loved had finally returned and had declared her love for him. He didn't care about the business right now. Remington had done well at making the business successful and it could practically run itself for months without his physical presence. He wanted every second with her so he could show her how much he loved her and cared for her and needed her before she found out about his run for mayor. There was no way to stop her from finding out, but he could make her see that he loved her and wouldn't do anything to hurt her. He needed her to see his omission was about protecting her—their love—the way she'd done for him all those years ago. He wanted her to never doubt his loyalty and commitment, despite some of his current actions.

"A penny for your thoughts, Mr. Krane."

Camille's angelic voice brought Remington out of his musings. It pleased him to find her arms wrapped tightly around his waist. He realized then that he had not yet commented on her demand that he go to work.

"Just thinking, Ladybug," he answered honestly and then kissed her on her forehead. "And I will go to work, but you have to promise to come by so I can introduce my employees to their new first lady." He'd said the last two words purposefully to hear them roll off his tongue. He liked the way they sounded. It was right that Camille be his first lady in everything he endeavored to do.

"Hmm…so tell me, Mr. Krane… I get to be your Michelle or am I more of a Beyonce type of first lady?"

"Don't make jokes because you won't know what to do if I give my answer." He smiled mischievously at Camille. "I could see you in pair of short cutoff shorts and—"

"Oh, you wish." Camille laughed and slapped Remi on the chest. "I'm talking National Anthem–singing Beyoncé so get your mind out of the gutter. The cut-offs don't leave the house." Camille bit her lip teasingly.

She didn't know what she was doing to him with her words and flirtations. And the idea of her walking around in cutoff shorts had him hard in seconds. He decided to put that information into his mental Rolodex. He'd have to convince her to wear those shorts and ask her to model them for him. But not now. Now he had to go to work.

He didn't want to go, but he had to because he knew the land deal was closing. He wanted to get the expansion of the Krane frozen foods division up and running before he left the company in the very capable hands of his Vice President while he pursued his political aspirations. He'd still be able to work with the company in an indirect capacity, but he didn't want to have to split too much of his time between the two positions if he won the election. He'd already come up with a plan to handle both and this land deal was the start of it.

Dammit, he had to go into the office.

Remington groaned because he knew he had to let her go. "Okay, I'll go to work, but since you're not wearing the shorts, I want to help you pick something out. I kind of liked assessing which thong I want to see you in for the day."

"No," Camille said while giggling. "Go or we'll never get out of here. I have plans and preparations to make. I have to talk to Anna. I have to call my building and break my lease. I have to hire movers. I have to talk to my dad…and then come out as Reese Elaine and—"

He stopped her. "I told you we're doing all of that together. There's no hurry. You're not going anywhere and Anna wants to wait anyway, so you have time. As long as no one else finds out, it will be fine. You've gone

this long and most people won't even question you staying around here with what happened with your father."

"Oh. My. God. Remington, we're engaged," Camille
squealed as if it just now dawned on her that she was
actually moving back to Fairdell to be with him. Then
another look marred her features and he recognized this
new emotion as panic. "Oh, my God. We're engaged.
This is completely crazy. In the few days I've been
here I lost my virginity, I decided to move back, I got
engaged and I'm changing how I've run my career for
years." And just as quickly as the panic started it subsided and the hysterical laughter started. Remi thought
maybe his wife-to-be was having a small breakdown
but it was just her way of working through everything.
She started mumbling sarcastically about how the people of Fairdell were going to *love* this new development
and how everyone in town probably already knew about
the engagement since Bernice Savage was there when
they told Camille's father. Camille was sure she'd be
called every name but a child of God for coming back
and taking the prodigal son off the market—Camille's
words not his—and exposing the religious little town to
the pornography of her books—also her words, not his.

"Where are they with the paperwork on the land
deal? How soon can I expect to hear from the owners?"
This was the most recent question Remington had posed
to Sonya Brandt, the company's lawyer.

"I called Franklin Weir and he's assured me the paperwork will be in your hands to review by the end of
the week. He apologized for the holdup. He said he had

to do more research on the company and was satisfied with what he found, whatever that means."

"Good. I need to get this deal done and out of the way as soon as possible because—"

"Mayor, right?" Sonya said and placed a curvy hip on the edge of his desk. He ignored her subtle attempt to be nice to him and focused on the fact that she seemed to know more than she was saying. "I heard your petition got approved."

"Well, you shouldn't have heard since I haven't given the approval for the information to be released. There are some issues I need to take care of before I make that information public knowledge. I'd appreciate it if you kept it to yourself since it took some convincing to get the office to keep it on their desk for a few extra days."

"May I ask why you don't want anyone to know?"

"You can ask, Sonya, but just like I don't want anyone to know about the petition, I am not ready to disclose those reasons, either."

Sonya looked a little put off by his response but quickly fixed her expression. "Would I be correct in assuming this has everything to do with Camille Ryan?" Sonya asked with a hint of malice lacing her words.

Remington didn't like the tone of Sonya's voice but he couldn't help the smile that took over his face. It was none of her business what he chose to do with his life and if she was in some way jealous or felt threatened by Camille, there was no need to be because Sonya had no claim to Remington. What they'd done was a onetime thing and it had happened nearly a decade ago when he was hurting and vulnerable after Camille's disappear-

ance from his life. It wasn't his fault that she somehow
thought they were on the road to fulfilling some man-
ufactured destiny their parents had in mind for them.
He'd already told Sonya long ago that they didn't have
a future regardless of what his grandfather thought.
He didn't love Sonya...hell, sometimes he could barely
stand her, especially when she got like this. She was a
beautiful girl, but her sometimes manipulative, often
entitled, attitude was a complete turnoff.

"Can I say something to you...as a friend and not
your lawyer?" Remi didn't say anything; he waited for
the unsolicited advice that he knew Sonya would im-
part regardless of how he answered her question. "She's
going to do it to you again. She left you once and as
soon as you get too serious she'll leave you again. She
tries to play innocent but she is...she is...you know she
writes this really smutty stuff and tries to pawn it off
as literature. You don't need that! What will everyone
say about you when you run for mayor? She'll destroy
you, your reputation and this company, and you don't
need that, Remi."

Remi felt he'd given her enough leeway. She was loud
and insulting and she had somehow found out about
Camille's career.

"How did you find out about her writing?" Remi had
jumped from his chair and walked around the desk. He
needed to get away from Sonya.

"I have my ways." The woman was now crossing
the line. She knew she had something to bargain with
and he could see the wheels in her head turning. She'd

ask for something he wasn't willing to give. Remington was sure of that.

So he waited for her to make her move. He knew she would because she would never pass on an opportunity like this. She'd definitely try to take advantage. And he was right. Sonya approached and leaned into Remi. With her height and heels they were almost eye-to-eye. Once she was a breath away Remi clenched his jaw and waited for her to make her demand.

"What do you want, Sonya? If I know anything about you, you've been sitting on this, waiting for the right moment, so out with it…what do you want?"

She rubbed her breasts against him, making it obvious what she desired. "Material possessions aren't quite what I had in mind, though I think a piece of the designer luggage I was looking at the other day could come in handy for when you invite me to your place to…" She trailed off and then made sure her eyes said exactly what would happen if he ever extended her an invitation, which would never happen.

Remi backed away. "I'm engaged. And as I've told you before—"

"He doesn't want you so why don't you back off, Sonya."

At the sound of Camille's voice, Remi nearly gasped. He hadn't even heard the door open.

"He's taken…officially," Camille said with a force he'd never heard from her before. She then held up her hand so Sonya could see the diamond in the antique setting on her finger. Then she stepped in between them, giving Sonya a view of her back.

Remi was thankful Camille had arrived.

"What are you doing here so early, Ladybug?" Remi couldn't resist touching her as she stood there. It was as if her body called out to him. He smoothed a hand over her hair and nearly forgot all about Sonya standing there until she cleared her throat.

"I think I will leave you two alone," Sonya said, obviously put out by Camille's presence. "Remi, we'll finish our conversation later."

"No, we're done. Just make sure you keep me updated on the information coming in from Franklin Weir."

Remi then gave his full attention to the woman who was now looking quite suspicious. Remi wasn't sure when exactly Camille had arrived, but he hoped she hadn't overheard about his petition to run for mayor.

"You want to tell me what that was about?"

"It was just Sonya being Sonya. I told her about us being engaged and she didn't take it well. But enough about her. Let me look at my future first lady. I'm glad you found my office okay. You didn't have any problems with security, did you? I told them to send you right up when you got here."

If Remi was trying to keep Camille from being suspicious with his uncharacteristic ramble, then he was sadly mistaken. She knew she wasn't crazy. She'd seen how close Remi and Sonya were when she walked in, but had only caught the end of what had been said. She didn't think Remi would be so bold as to invite Camille to his office *and* have a fling with his company attorney all in the same day, so she believed what he'd told her about Sonya not taking their engagement well. It was understandable since the woman had been led to believe she had some sort of claim on Camille's fiancé all these years.

The woman was not to be trusted and Camille could definitely see Sonya trying to proposition Remi just to test his loyalty. Camille was jealous but decided not to act like the typical jealous girlfriend. She'd made her point and would just let Remi handle Sonya. It appeared he'd been doing that when Camille walked into his office.

"You're not a rambler, Remi, so something else must've gone on here besides—"

"Camille, you know I'd never do—"

Camille laughed, amused by the way he immediately thought she was about to confront him about what she walked in on. "Not what I meant, but good to know that you'd never let her influence you. I was trying to say that I know you're holding out on me. You look... unsettled."

"She knows about Reese Elaine," he blurted and looked directly into her eyes. Camille wasn't sure what he was saying. "What do you mean? How could she know?" Camille was at a loss, but it didn't surprise her in the least. Sonya was always determined when it came to something she wanted, even if it took using unconventional methods to get it.

"Not sure, but that's not really the important part." Remi shifted as though he was uncomfortable with telling Camille about Sonya's behavior even though it was obvious Sonya was up to *something* when Camille had walked into Remi's office. "Sonya thinks I'll sleep with her to keep your secret," Remington blurted, looking the slightest bit guilty. But he had no reason to be. Camille had heard him turn Sonya down without hesitation.

Camille was actually surprised by Sonya. She knew the woman suffered from a sense of entitlement, but didn't think she'd try to ever force a man to be with her. It wasn't as if Sonya wasn't beautiful enough to get her own man. It made Camille feel sorry for Sonya because there had to be another reason for the woman's desperation. She just hoped Sonya would figure it out and leave Remi alone.

This was unexpected. She had known there would be people who wouldn't understand what she wrote about but someone as young and as brazen as Sonya should surely be sophisticated enough to understand her writing was art.

However, Camille had pissed Sonya off and Remi had rejected her, so Sonya would definitely cash in on this information regardless of whether or not she understood the need to keep it quiet. Whom she'd run crying injustice to first, Camille did not know, but she knew she'd run.

"What do we do?" she asked Remi.

"We wait. There's nothing else to do. I don't want to worry about her. You can call Anna later and warn her and maybe she can push everything up somehow. But you know that means the talk with your father has to be sooner rather than later."

"I know."

"Don't worry about any of that. You look beautiful and this white dress…perfect. Makes me wonder what you'll look like in your wedding dress."

Could this man be any more wonderful? He was not at all afraid to tell Camille how he felt about her. She loved his possessiveness, his constant need to touch her, the way he looked at her as if he wanted her every minute of every day. And he was all hers. He'd turned down sex with the wealthy, beautiful, experienced Sonya Brandt because *she* was the only one he wanted. She'd never find anyone more loyal to her. She'd never find anyone more honest. *Really…what man confesses to his fiancée that a gorgeous woman propositioned him?*

"What makes you think I'm wearing white?" she teased him. "Maybe you've had me doing such naughty things that I am no longer worthy of being sheathed in such an innocent color."

Remi peeled her purse strap from her shoulder and set it on his desk. He then pushed her hair off her shoulders and let it fall behind her. His fingers threaded into her hair. "I want you in white. This body," he whispered as if they weren't alone, "has only been touched by me." A hand on her hip and a soft squeeze there made her need to stifle a moan. "That is the biggest turn-on," he admitted and then kissed her below her ear. "Only me." The kisses continued down her neck until he could go no further because of the cut of her dress. "White."

It was a one-word demand, not a suggestion, not a question. It wasn't harsh, though. It was almost seductive. She wasn't sure how one word, a color at that, could be seductive, but the way Remington Krane demanded her body be encased in white on their wedding day made her want to run out and try on every stark white dress she could lay her hands on.

When she thought he would take her mouth roughly under his, he didn't. He began slowly, gently stoking the embers of her desire. He barely grazed her lips with his own and the whisper of breath that filled the space between them was almost more than Camille could bear. Her whole being seemed to fill and begin to spill over with want and she could no longer stand the wait to be his again.

Remi's lips finally joined with hers, but only a feathery brush, not nearly enough, given the way she was dripping with need. His teasing was almost arrogant in its manner, yet it was still all about her and making sure she was the center of his world in that moment.

Camille allowed Remi to lead her because surely if she held any amount of control in this situation, they'd already be spread out naked on top of his desk.

The kiss deepened and when she could no longer hold in her moan, he took advantage, sliding his tongue into her mouth, tentatively exploring and caressing with a masterful tenderness. And now his roaming hands had her blood pounding in her brain, the feel of them had her heart nearly leaping from her chest, and his skilled mouth had her writhing against him like she was in heat.

"White it is," Camille finally said when they had no choice but to pull away from one another or pass out from lack of oxygen.

"Mmm…" Remi groaned through clenched teeth. "I

don't want to share you. You are looking too damn hot right now." Remi pulled away reluctantly. "But I want to show you off. Plus, I think David wants to see you." He chuckled when he mentioned his friend. "I think he might cry when he finds out we're engaged."

Chapter 16

The dress Camille wore to Remi's office spoke to his more primal instincts. It was a conservatively short white number with little raised ridges in the fabric that were interesting to touch. It was fitted at the top, but at her waist it flared out into a bouncy skirt. There was nothing revealing about the garment. The neckline was modest, the sleeves came to her elbows, but the hemline…well, she obviously came here to tease and taunt him or to have him take her right here in his office. He hoped both the former *and* the latter were true because he was already hard enough to hammer nails.

She knew his weakness. Her legs. The fact that such a petite woman could have such long legs amazed him. Beautiful, glowing, toned, thick, sculpted, soft, smooth, bronzed legs. And the crazy part was he was not even a leg man. He was a definite fan of the curvier rear portion of women. Camille had both. She had the most perfect rear atop an equally perfect set of legs. And now that he'd seen her in heels… Let's just say he'd have to buy her a closet full of dresses because none would survive his potent need for her. If he got his hands on her after a night of enjoying the sight of her feminine and graceful limbs move and flex inside a pair of four-inch heels, he'd destroy whatever barrier was between them, even if it was a thousand-dollar dress.

Reining himself in after their tension-filled kiss, Remi sent Camille into his personal bathroom so she could freshen up. He needed her out of his sight so he could calm down. Something about her scent when she was aroused called to him—almost like each tantalizing note was engineered just to tease his senses. It was distracting in the best kind of way.

The tour and introductions went very well. Camille was a hit with everyone. And since a lot of the people who worked for him were young, they didn't know about Camille or that she'd left all those years ago. Her worry that the women wouldn't like her was unfounded as she was nice and personable. Remi was astounded by the easy way she interacted with everyone. She pointed out pictures on some of the desks, school memorabilia, and even commented on a few quotes one young woman had decorating her space. She complimented women on clothes and knew where they'd bought certain items. She had the men adjusting their slacks left and right. It could have made him jealous but it didn't because each and every time any man flirted or they moved to the next floor of the building, she'd look at him lovingly or steal a kiss in the elevator.

He was glad he didn't tell her there were cameras in there.

They skipped visiting Sonya's office and made a bee-line for David's. They found him doing his usual stress-relieving activity, making origami shapes. He'd been doing it since he met a girl who had the same hobby. He'd said she was weird and boring but for some reason he was compelled to actually try to fold one shape after watching a video and had become hooked. He had books on the subject, subscribed to some sort of magazine, and participated in online groups that shared rare and unusual shapes and techniques. Remi always found it funny that David didn't realize he'd turned into the woman he'd dumped for being weird.

His stress level must've been unusually high today because there were already a few shapes completed and it was barely lunchtime.

When David saw Camille he straightened in his chair and swept the shapes onto the floor at his feet. Camille probably didn't notice the move but Remi did and he had to chuckle because the three shapes on his desk were a drop in the bucket compared to the shelf he had lined with his creations. Remi could admit that the man was good at his hobby though his complete immersion in it was still a mystery.

"I see you couldn't stay away," David said to Camille. "I'm so glad you had this chump bring you to me. Did he tell you I asked about you?"

Camille actually blushed when Dave flirted, and

though Remi knew he had no reason to feel it, a flash of jealousy shot through his body and he latched possessively onto Camille's waist.

"It's good to see you as well, David. But sorry… this guy here has taken me off the market." Camille shrugged and briefly flashed her left hand and wiggled her fingers. She tried to appear nonchalant but she couldn't contain her smile. Her full, pink, glossy lips curved softly upward and he felt a throb in his pants when she lifted her head to him and winked.

"Ho-ly crap. Congratulations," David said seriously and got up from his chair to hug them both at the same time. It was just David's way. He was extra excited and jovial about everything, which made him good at his job. When he let go of the couple, he exclaimed, "I'm throwing you two a party. We're inviting the whole damn town. The Prince of Fairdell Weds." David said it as if he was reading a headline in the local newspaper. "This is going to be like Will and Kate coming to Fairdell to live," he said, and Camille laughed at the man's histrionics.

To Remi's surprise Camille agreed. "Sounds like it'll be a good time. I'm looking forward to a party thrown by you, David." The even more surprising part was that Remi could tell that she was being honest. She actually wanted to share their happiness with her family and friends and even those who may not like her too much. It showed her heart. It showed that she was willing to try to put hard feelings behind her and move forward. After all, she had to live there so why not try and make life more peaceful by extending an olive branch.

David started to throw out party ideas until his office phone rang. It was his assistant telling him the call he'd been expecting had finally come through. David took the call and Remi and Camille left. They decided to take the stairs since Remi's office was only one floor above the one they were on. He could hardly wait to get her alone.

They'd traveled up the first set of stairs and were on the second set when Remi turned Camille and pressed her into the wall. "Thank you."

"Why are you thanking me? I didn't do anything." Her voice was small and despite the dialogue going on right now, her body and eyes were having their own conversation with him. She hoped he was paying attention.

"You didn't have to agree to the party, but you did. I think it'll be a good thing," Remi said and snaked his hand under the hem of her dress. He kept talking as if his hand wasn't roaming her curves underneath the dress. But she heard none of what he said.

"I want…I want to include everyone who wants to be involved. You're right, it should be…" Her words trailed off and her head lightly thudded against the wall behind her when his hand slid into her white thong and ripped it free.

"Should be what, baby?" He liked this. This pretending that they weren't in the stairwell about to have sex. He liked that she still tried to play along and continue the conversation even though it was getting harder and harder for her to speak through her arousal.

Remi took their game one step further and pressed his thumb firmly onto her nub and simultaneously plunged two fingers into her.

"It should be fun, Remi! Ohhhh..." she uttered over and over in a loud whisper that was cute as well as filled with desire. He got pleasure from the feel of her tightening around his fingers and the gentle suction sound of her wetness echoing in the space.

No longer wanting to play the game or keep up conversation about anything other than what he was about to do to her, Remi whispered, "You do understand that I am about to take you right here against this wall, right?" No real response came. Only a gasp that he swallowed whole. "Arms around my neck. Legs around my waist, Ladybug." His orders were clear and concise and she obeyed without hesitation. It was some sort of record that he was able to free the erection that had been cursing him for waiting for so long to have her.

They both released a sigh when he slid into her. It was a moment they always seemed to relish, when their bodies first joined. Once the moment passed, Remi began moving, slowly at first, then more quickly. The increase in speed must've done something to Camille because her back arched off the wall and her nails dug into his shoulders as her body shuddered. She convulsed around his invasion, triggering his release deep into her womb.

As an afterthought Camille noticed they were in a very public stairwell and cursed their lack of control, but Remi knew she was only half-serious since the smile never left her face.

After their quickie on the stairwell, Remi and Camille were finally able to fit lunch into their day. They
ate in his office and flirted and talked about their time
apart until Remi's next meeting. He instructed Camille
to keep the car he'd let her use for the rest of the day
and to return to get him so they could have dinner and
he'd leave the car he'd driven behind. What he didn't
tell her was that he was taking her to the country club
to tell his grandfather about their engagement. There
was a good chance the man already knew, but telling
him in person was the proper thing to do if Remi were
going to have any chance of getting the old man's approval. Not that he needed it, but it would be nice to
have support from the only family he had left.

Camille had no idea what to do with herself for the
hours till she picked up Remi. She felt slightly uncomfortable riding around in his car so she decided to go by
the house and check on her father. He'd been fine and
had basically returned to doing what he'd done before
the trouble with his heart.

Pulling up in the driveway, Camille saw an unfamil-
iar car. Upon closer inspection she saw that the vehicle had a sticker on the back from a well-known rental
car company. However, as soon as the door to Remi's
Mercedes closed, the door to the house flew open and a
half-black, half-Armenian woman pranced out looking
as expensive and put-together as the last time Camille
had laid eyes on her.

"Wow…look at you. Getting rid of your v-card certainly agrees with you, doesn't it?" the fast-talking

Anna quipped when they were about a foot from one another. The pair hugged as if they had not seen each other only a week ago.

"What are you doing here? Not that I mind, but I thought you had some business to take care of first." They walked to the house as they talked. "If you had called me, you wouldn't have had to wait here for me."

Anna, being her usual crazy self, uttered, "I didn't mind waiting here for you. You didn't tell me your father was sexy as sin. Goodness, Camille, now I know why he's so popular with the local old bats. I may have to give them a run for their money. Never been into older guys, but there's a first time for everything."

"First of all...eww! And secondly...why would the words *my father is sexy as sin* ever leave my mouth? And lastly...I don't put anything past you, but I don't know how I'd handle you being my stepmom. That would be weird." They both laughed. They both felt that Anna was a sort of surrogate aunt to Camille. She was seven years older than Camille but had the heart and disposition of an eighteen-year-old. There was no doubt that if her agent thought Camille's father would return her affections, she'd try her hand at getting him. It was disturbing and funny at the same time.

Once they were inside they chatted for a while, until Camille's father emerged from the backyard with his hands covered in some sort of black substance.

"Oh, hey, Bug. I was just starting the grill. Your friend here said she's never had pork steaks. You know it's my specialty on the grill so I thought I'd throw a few on," her father said, smiling as if he'd just opened a new toy or was *about* to open one. That smile had surely been induced by Anna's flirting and when Camille looked to her for confirmation, Anna shrugged and then winked. Camille had to roll her eyes.

"Hmm…that's interesting since I don't think I have ever seen her eat anything other than chicken or fish. I guess she wants to try something new, Daddy," Camille said to her father's back as he went heading upstairs to shower while the food cooked.

Once she thought her father was out of earshot, Camille fell out laughing and Anna joined her. "What did you do to him? I've never seen him this happy to grill pork."

"Nothing. I just talked to him. You know, like an equal, not like the father of one of my clients."

"Clients? Bug, what is she talking about?" Reese Ryan asked from the staircase. "What does Anna do for you?"

"Daddy… I thought you were going to shower?" Camille said, not answering the question.

"Camille Elise Ryan, I have taught you better than to lie to me."

Anna chuckled at her being chastised like a toddler and Camille winced at her whole name being called out. "Okay, Daddy. Camille is my agent. She manages my writing career," she announced abruptly. Camille felt small as she sat on the worn couch in her living room. Her father loomed above her as he stood on the first step of the staircase. But when she'd expected to see confusion laced in his features, there was…understanding.

"I haven't worked at a school in years. I have been

writing for some time now and have done well with it. I am actually kind of big deal, although no one knows who I am. I write…I write stuff that you and the people in this town may see as offensive or dirty. That's why I didn't tell you. That's why I didn't tell anyone. I wanted you to be able to live a life free of the stigma that came with my writing. I didn't want you to lose business because of what I did for a living so I let you believe I was still teaching. No one knows about my writing. No one knows my face. They only know my pseudonym. I'd planned to tell you all this once I figured out how. There are some things changing and…" Camille then turned to Anna, "and some people may already know."

"Is that why your 'friend' Anna is here? To help you with the fallout from revealing that you are Reese Elaine?"

Wait! What did he just say? Did I mention that during my rant? "Did you just call me Reese Elaine? How… You knew?"

Her father nodded and then smiled.. "Yes, I know, Bug. I've known for a while and was just waiting until you felt comfortable enough to tell me." He seemed to forget all about the shower he was about to take as he leaned back on the step he sat on. "It's hard not to pick up a book that has your and your deceased wife's name on the cover in big bold letters. I saw the book when I had to have some tests done in Atlanta. I stopped to get coffee in a bookstore and saw your book as I waited in line. I wasn't positive it was you until I read the back cover. It said something along the lines of you being raised in a small town by your single father. It said you

were a girly girl with tomboy tendencies and I immediately knew it was you. That was what Remi always
said about you—the part about you being a girly tomboy. I think I cried right then and there I was so proud
of you. But I also understood why you had not told me
and it made me even prouder that you'd sacrifice the
recognition to protect me, to protect Remi, to protect
the town you were raised in. But no more. My daughter is a famous author and I want everyone to know it.
I don't care what these hypocrites around here say. You
got me and Remi and Charlie and Anna on your side.
Ain't that right, Anna?"

"Damn right. Reese and I are here to make sure this
coming-out party goes smooth as silk. Speaking of
which…who are these people who already know about
Reese Elaine?"

Camille went on to tell her how Sonya Brandt had
somehow found out and had tried to blackmail Remi.
Anna and Reese both cursed a few times when they
heard what Sonya had done. Given how popular Camille's books were, it would create a firestorm in the
press if this wasn't revealed properly. Media would de-
scend on the town, the townspeople would blame Camille for the disruption and Sonya would get a sick
satisfaction out of it all. Camille would have no choice
but to give Remi up if that happened and she really
wasn't ready to do that. She'd never be ready to give him
up again. But if it meant protecting him once again…
Camille shook away the morbid thought. She couldn't
entertain the negative. It was too late for that now.

"Okay…I have an idea and I hope you like it," Anna

proclaimed, and when she was done explaining the idea, Camille was completely on board. Hadn't she just agreed to something similar earlier? Maybe she could get Anna and David together since he knew the people of Fairdell and she knew how to plan a great party.

Chapter 17

"Are you sure you're going to be okay staying here? Remi has plenty of room at his place and—"

"Nonsense," Anna exclaimed. "I'd never think of coming in between your constant 'celebrating.'" She wiggled her eyebrows at the word. "Girl, you have been a virgin for too long and you need to be getting some morning, noon and night to make up for lost time. Plus, why would I pass up staying with a man who cooks for me? Never in my thirty-five years has a man cooked for me. I plan to enjoy every minute. By the time you come back around, I'll be your new stepmom," Anna said with a flourish and pushed Camille toward Remi's car.

"Okay. But don't— Never mind. He's a grown man and he can take care of himself. Just don't tell me about it if you…you know."

"You know me, Camille. I *always* kiss and tell so don't push your luck thinking I'll hold out because your father is the one who sexed me up."

"Thanks for that visual." She shook her head as if to dispel the image. "I'm going now. Behave. I'll call after dinner and we'll start planning."

"By the time you get back I'll have this thing planned and the invitations mailed. But thanks for that guy's number. Some local help will be appreciated," Anna yelled from the doorway as Camille opened the car door.

Camille didn't worry about Anna or her father. The woman was grown and so was her father. If he went there, that was his business. And if Anna let him then that was hers. Camille never stopped her father from being a man just because he was a single father. Anna was sweet and funny and a great woman who sort of reminded her of the way people had described her mother. A free spirit. They'd said Elaine Ryan wasn't afraid to speak her mind and she wasn't afraid to go after the man her family had said wasn't good enough for her.

She called Remi when she reached his office building. "Hey, Remi, I'm here. Did you want me to come up?"

He declined, telling her to park in his grandfather's reserved space and that he'd meet her there. Camille sat in the car and waited patiently. She decided to check her makeup in the mirror as she wondered where Remi could possibly be taking her for dinner. Her outfit was not one for the drive-through and there were only a few places in Fairdell that warranted such attire. She figured that maybe there had been some new establishments built that she had yet to see, so she relaxed and waited.

A few minutes later there was a knock on the window. She turned and smiled, but then her smile fell away when she realized it was Sonya standing there. Instead of rolling down the window, Camille opened the door and stepped out. She was sure there'd be a confrontation and she needed to be on somewhat equal footing.

"What can I help you with, Sonya? I'm pretty sure we have nothing else to say to one another."

"That's where you're wrong, *Ladybug*." The term of endearment came out like an insult. "But since you want to be mean to me, I'll let you find out on your own. Oh, who am I kidding? I'd love to see you squirm," Sonya said and smiled. "Don't you think Remington Krane would make a great mayor of our little town? I think so." Sonya started to walk off. "Oh, and nice ring." She chuckled as if she knew something Camille didn't.

What was that all about? Camille assumed it was just the woman's jealous nature. As Remi had said before, it was just Sonya being Sonya. And whatever she was talking about didn't make sense anyway. What did her thoughts about who should be Fairdell's next mayor have to do with Remi? Surely if he still had those aspirations, he'd have mentioned them to her before he'd asked her to marry him. Him running for office was something important—something they'd discussed as teens. It was also something he couldn't do if Camille was his wife. There was no way he could be mayor of Fairdell—the city where going to church on Sunday was nearly a requirement—and be married to a woman who wrote erotica. He knew her reasoning for leaving town the first time and wouldn't do something as deceitful as keeping things from her just so he could trap her into staying.

No, Sonya was just jealous, Camille told herself and tried to purge the doubts from her mind before Remi arrived. She decided to keep their little encounter to herself since she had no reason to doubt Remi. He'd been nothing but good to her.

"Hey, baby, you look deep in thought," Remi crooned, snatching her away from her inner musings. She'd been so lost in thought she hadn't heard him approach. His arms found their way around her waist and he leaned into her back and kissed her ear.

"Just thinking. I had to tell my father," Camille said, hoping that statement would cover up her being off balance. She didn't want to admit that Sonya had gotten to her. Camille then robotically pulled away from Remi but he wasn't having any part of that.

"Hold on there, Ladybug. I thought we were going to tell him together." Remi's hands moved to her hips to stop her from backing away. He bent down and searched her face for something, but she had no idea what.

"When I say I told him, I use those words loosely. He actually overheard me and Anna talking about it, but when I thought I'd have to explain and get him to understand, I found out I didn't have to. He already knew and had been waiting for me to tell him." She went on to recall the story her father had told her.

"Well, that's good, isn't it? So why don't you look like you feel better?"

"I do feel better. I think I'm still a little thrown off from the whole conversation, that's all." It was the truth, but she had not told him which conversation had thrown her off. It wasn't the one with her father, which had gone well. She was talking about the very brief confrontation she'd just had with Sonya.

"Maybe there is something I can do to make you forget and focus on having a fantastic dinner."

Remi's constant interest in her was flattering to say the least. But it was so much more than that. When he was around, she needed to be touched by him and if they couldn't touch, she needed him near. It was crazy for her to feel that way after spending ten years happily alone. Maybe that said something about her view of happiness. She probably had not been happy—not completely anyway. Now she was on the way to having everything she wanted. Camille decided to push the doubt away and revel in the indisputable euphoria over the changes occurring in her life.

"What did you have in mind?" Camille finally relaxed and decided to just let things happen. The wheels had already been set in motion for a marriage, a move and a coming out and she didn't think she'd go back if she could. She was on this course and she'd ride it out and see where it led.

"Hmm…I'm thinking," Remi said and kissed Camille on her forehead, not moving his lips until it was time to speak again. Camille leaned into his hard chest and sought comfort there. The deeply ridged muscles of his abs clenched when she hooked her fingers into the waistband of his belted designer slacks. "I like the way you think, baby, but I'm the one that's supposed to be coming up with the ideas here so don't you dare move another muscle or so help me I will take you right here, right now up against my Mercedes."

Could mere words make a woman come? Camille had no idea that it was possible, but just the sound of his voice had turned her core to mush and she now felt as if she'd fallen over a cliff bound for ecstasy.

Camille closed her eyes and waited for whatever he intended to do. She felt the shadow of his much larger body descending, taking the light filtering through her closed eyelids away as he got closer. Camille shivered with anticipation when she felt his warm, minty breath graze her ear. "Mission accomplished," he whispered and then stood back to his full height as if he wasn't just as ready to jump her as she was him. She was slightly disoriented as she tried to figure what those two words could've meant; then it dawned on her.

It had worked. He'd accomplished his mission to make her forget all about her little confrontation with Sonya. She then watched him as he flashed his perfectly straight, white teeth at her with as much arrogance as he could muster in a smile. He then helped her into the passenger seat and declared he was about to feed his woman.

It didn't take long for Camille to realize where they were going. To Remi's grandfather. She didn't say a word because she didn't have to. It was inevitable, she figured, so why not today? She was sure Frederick Krane would not be happy about either her writing career or their engagement so she prepared for the oncoming disdain.

* * *

Remi had to give it to Camille. She kept her composure as they pulled through the gates of Fairdell Country Club. She was not a fan of this place, though she'd spent quite a bit of time there. Her father's company was contracted to landscape the property and she often accompanied him there on days when Remi begged her to do so, saying he'd be there, as well.

They pulled up to the valet and Remi hurried around to the other side. He was a little nervous that Camille had yet to say anything about where they were. He hoped she was just trying to mentally prepare herself for the encounter.

He offered his hand to her and as he pulled her close she whispered through clenched teeth, "You owe me big time for this one. I mean *really* big. Think polishing toenails kind of big, buddy."

He chuckled because he'd told her that he'd have to be hypnotized by a woman until he was unable to think straight before he would do something like polish a woman's toes. For him that was a definite man-law violation, but something about her made him consider giving in. Hell, he'd give her a full pedicure and kiss each toe afterward if she let him.

He was just that far gone.

"No problem. Now let's go. The king awaits," he joked and he liked that she smiled at the barb. She'd be fine. He wouldn't allow his grandfather to berate her. She was his fiancée now and whether the old man accepted it or not, it wouldn't change Remi's mind in any way.

They were greeted in a matter of seconds after walking through the lobby and over to the waiting hostess.

"Hello, Remi, I mean Mr. Krane. You grandfather is already seated. Follow me."

The young woman smiled and flirted with him as she led them to the table, which wasn't a first. Remi did his best as he always did to ignore the woman's rudeness and unprofessionalism so as not to make a scene. But the way she ignored Camille's presence, by not greeting her properly as she should've, rubbed Remi the wrong way. He'd have a word with her boss because Camille would soon be his wife and he wouldn't stand for her to be treated any differently than he was treated as a member.

His grandfather always sat at the same table so the man would not be hard to find. Sure enough, Remi found him sitting in the middle of the dining area where he had a view of everyone going in or out. There was at least a one-yard radius around his table so no one would walk too close unless he called them over.

Frederick Krane did not look surprised to see Camille and Remi walk in together. Remi figured someone had gotten back to him. If the person was who he thought it was, then Remi's grandfather more than likely knew about Camille being Reese Elaine as well as their engagement. It would make this meeting that much more difficult. No doubt Frederick would already be prepared to battle with Remi over what he'd see as a mistake Remington was making with the run for mayor on the line.

What Remington did not expect in a million years

was for Frederick Krane to stand and greet Camille with a smile and a hug. He even kissed her on the cheek and told her he was happy that he'd soon have her as a granddaughter.

Am I dreaming?

"What are you up to, Granddad?"

"Why must I be up to anything, Remington? I am happy that you have finally come to your senses and asked this vision in white to marry you. Camille will be a great addition to the Krane family."

Camille appeared to be as stunned as Remi. She stood there as if she was trying to figure out if she was imagining all this, as well. He'd seen Frederick when the man was happy. The man didn't get happy about many things except for money, power, status and the occasional attention from one of the ladies at church. If his motives didn't fall into one of those categories, then he had to have fallen and bumped his head because he seemed to be on cloud nine.

Then his grandfather chuckled. *Chuckled?* Remi *had* to be dreaming because he didn't think he'd ever heard the man laugh. He'd seen him smile sinisterly after taking down a business adversary, but he'd never seen the man like this.

Something wasn't right; Remi just had to figure out what that was.

"Have a seat." Frederick gestured to the empty chairs. "Champagne should be out soon. I told them we were celebrating having a bestselling author join our family. I told them that woman who wrote that Grey book is nothing compared to you. And get this...many of the women I spoke to already have at least one of your books on their shelf. At first they were a little shy about admitting it—you know, with the type of books they are," he whispered, "but one brave soul was unafraid and told me my future granddaughter will be worth twice as much when she finally reveals who she really is. Camille Ryan Krane better known as Reese Elaine." He turned to Remi. "You have done well. I approve and so will everyone else in the town if I have anything to say about it," he said with confidence and authority.

What the hell...? I should probably grab Camille's hand and get up and run before the alien invading my grandfather's body explodes through his chest and turns them into— So maybe he and Camille should not have watched that alien movie last night. This was not the time for him to be cracking mentally. He had to stay alert because now that his grandfather's words had sunk in, he looked up and glared at the man.

"Granddad, Camille is not some commodity or asset. I love her and we're getting married for love, not to boost the Krane name. I would have married Camille regardless of whether she was Reese Elaine or the school teacher I thought she was all these years."

At his words Camille squeezed their already joined hands. They let that statement digest as their waiter poured the champagne.

"I didn't mean for it to sound that way, Remington," his grandfather said when the waiter had departed. "I only meant to show you how proud I am of you and Camille. When Miss Brandt informed me of the new developments in your life, I admit, at first I was skeptical.

But then she started to show me evidence of who Reese Elaine was." The man then turned to Camille. His face became a mask of sincerity that even convinced Remi. "You are very good at what you do, dear. Do not allow anyone to let you feel ashamed for writing about a subject that is as old as time. Maybe you'll even stir up a few of these old bats around here." Then he laughed at his own joke.

"Uh…thank you? I—"

"Let me say this and then maybe you will feel more comfortable and trust that I want us to start over for Remi's sake and for his happiness." Frederick straightened and surprised Remi by taking Camille's hand in his. "I am very sorry, Camille. I am an old man who was stuck in his ways. I judged you and you didn't deserve it. You graduated number three in your class in high school and received highest honors in your upper level degrees. You are an exceptional woman and Remington is lucky to have you by his side." He then turned back to Remington and said, "We'll figure out the rest, son." Remi knew those words had everything to do with the election and he was glad his grandfather didn't elaborate on it. It seemed he and Camille had another ally— one that would surely be able to convince the town that his grandson's future wife was special and good and shouldn't be defined by the words in her books.

"Thank you, Mr. Krane," Camille said. She beamed, taking the comments to heart. Remi could still see the caution in the depths of her brown eyes but she was remarkable in her ability to push that aside and just accept things as they came.

"Call me Granddad."

And she did. For the rest of the meal. Since they had no announcement to make, they had a pleasant dinner. His grandfather asked questions about Camille's career that were not out of line in any way. He complimented her on getting the job at the private school so soon after graduating, but told her that he was glad she chose the path she did. Of course he would say that considering that path led her to being a possible millionaire if she wasn't one already. Dollars and cents were something his grandfather respected, especially if wealth came from hard work and determination.

Remi was surprised once again when the old man would not take no for an answer when he offered to pay for the wedding. And it surprised him even more when his grandfather actually shed a tear when he lamented that Remi's parents and grandmother were not there to see this day.

It was hard to determine which of his grandfather's feelings were real and which were a façade since he did such a good job of mingling the two. Remi had no doubt that the man would use Camille's name for his own gain in some way. He was the type of man who looked at the bottom line and if she was as successful as Remi thought, then Camille Ryan was a star in Frederick Krane's eyes. Remi doubted if they'd have any problems out of the man again.

Chapter 18

Later that night Camille lounged on a mound of pillows while Remi concentrated on not getting light pink nail polish on the skin surrounding her toenails. The dinner with Remington's grandfather had not been an ordeal at all, but her fiancé insisted on doing this for her and she graciously accepted. She didn't think she could turn him down anyway because her body felt like a mound of jelly after he'd massaged her from head to toe when they'd arrived back at his house.

She'd tried to convince Remi to take her home, saying she shouldn't keep leaving her father alone, but he said he'd already texted her father and Reese was enjoying Anna's company. Camille didn't want to think about what that meant, so she agreed to go with Remi. She wasn't dumb enough to walk in on *that*. Her father was not yet fifty and Anna was thirty-five. She would not play mother hen to two adults.

After the massage he'd carried her to the shower and had washed away the oils he'd used. He'd cleaned every inch of her with a gentle touch. He'd kissed her body all over. He'd then brought her to climax with his skilled tongue and had refused to take her when she'd begged for him to be inside her.

Camille had argued that it wasn't right to leave him in such a state, but he'd adamantly refused. He had wanted the night to be all about her. She would've thought he was guilty of something if she didn't know better. But she quickly brushed that ridiculous thought aside.

"All done," Remi finally declared and Camille wiggled her perfectly polished pink toes.

"Come here. I need to thank you with a kiss."

"I accept that offer," he playfully commented and then moved to hover over her body. The kiss he placed on her lips was soft and sweet. So was the next kiss that landed at the spot where her robe revealed just a bit of glowing bronzed cleavage. Then there was a tug at the tie on her robe and as much as she wanted him, she decided to play along with his earlier rule.

"Oh, no, you don't. No sex, remember? Your rule, not mine and I plan to adhere to it. Go ahead and shower. I'll think about changing my mind while you're in there."

"Fair enough. But maybe I can give you a little nudge in the right direction," Remi's smooth, deep voice crooned suggestively and Camille almost changed her mind instantly.

She wondered what he had in mind with that statement but didn't have to wait long. He stared directly at her, his eyes glazed with lust, and started to strip. His eyes never left hers as he relieved himself of his belt, pants, and underwear. Before she could enjoy the view, he removed the pinstriped button-down he already had partially unbuttoned. He was now standing there, in all his glory, completely naked. It was an image she'd be glad to have burned into her retinas forever.

Taking him in from the bottom and moving upward, Camille assessed the lean, chiseled muscles of his long legs until she reached the part of him that she wanted the most. His erection called to her and she licked her lips at the thought of what that particular organ could do to her. She regained her focus and marveled at the way his broad chest made her feel safe even at this distance and how his defined arms flexed when he moved.

She smiled when she got to the low-cut beard that framed his rugged, yet exquisitely molded jaw, knowing he kept the facial hair because she liked it. It was so manly and she loved when he purposely brushed the stubble against her thigh as he loved her from below. His smooth-shaven head was like a magnet to her hands and she loved to rub him there and listen to him hum softly because her ministrations against his scalp felt that good.

Though that whole assessment took only a moment, it had done its job in enticing her to change her mind. However, she wasn't ready to let him know that she'd caved so easily, so she pretended to not be affected by the smooth expanse of his mouth-watering caramel skin.

He sauntered off arrogantly when she appeared un-
moved, but the look he gave her was a knowing one.
She was sure he was aware she wouldn't be able to resist him much longer.

Only a few minutes had passed when she could no
longer take the wait. Camille hopped off the bed and
untied her robe, letting it fall to the floor. She made it
halfway to the bathroom door when her phone chimed
with a text. She'd check the message and continue on
her mission.

The message was a 911 from Anna that caused Camille's heart to skip a beat. Anna was with her father
and the only emergency she could fathom was one
where her father had been rushed back to the hospital
for returning to normal activities too soon. She quickly
called Anna. The call was one she'd never forget.

She looked toward the door of the bathroom the
whole time her friend spoke to her. With each statement Anna kept apologizing for having to tell her over
the phone but Camille barely heard the apology because
she was in shock. She felt so stupid for believing she
could come back and everything would be okay.

Remington had let her fall in love with him. He'd let
her say yes to his proposal. They'd discussed all sorts
of plans for their future during their pillow talk and not
once had he mentioned running for mayor.

It hurt her to think he felt he had to lie to her and
manipulate her. It felt as if their reunion was a lie. But
Camille knew Remington. His feelings for her were
genuine so his reason for not telling her couldn't have
been malicious. When she thought about it, his intent

was clear. He'd intended to risk his future, his political career, for her.

Maybe he didn't think he was taking a risk, but Camille was sure he was.

Camille had realized her dreams and wouldn't allow him to risk his for her. It was too late to turn back on revealing herself as Reese Elaine, but she wasn't yet married and could take that back. She may hurt Remi, but in the long run he'd appreciate her making this sacrifice once again.

It was the worst kind of déjà vu.

As Camille hastily dressed, she allowed Anna's words to run through her mind over and over. Her agent had said a letter had come by messenger addressed to Reese Elaine. Anna didn't have any problem opening the letter thinking it was probably about Camille's coming out since Anna had been expecting a few deliveries.

She'd opened the letter and seen Remington's completed, submitted petition to run for mayor. The stamped date had let Camille know Remington had been keeping secrets from her since the day she'd come back and they'd first laid eyes on one another. It was like a slap to her face knowing he didn't trust her enough to make her own decisions. But that thought had been fleeting. Remington was a good man and she knew that no matter how upset she got about the secret, he'd done it to protect her and the future they'd planned, as she'd done for him all those years ago. He knew Camille wouldn't want him to risk anything just so they could be together, but he was still willing to risk it all for their love. It was a flattering sentiment, but one Camille couldn't allow.

Finally dressed, she dashed from Remington's house and walked down the street to meet the cab she'd called. She thought as she walked and realized this was her fault. She should've been more cautious. She should've asked more questions. At twenty-eight she was still a little naive and had believed Remi when he'd agreed they'd be honest with one another from now on.

But now, as the cab pulled up to her home and she saw Anna standing there waiting for her, she felt a stab of pain in her heart. She'd never get the happily-ever-after she so often wrote in her books.

Remi thought Camille was playing some sort of game with him when he came out of the bathroom and saw that she was gone. He looked for her and called her name and chuckled at her antics. He thought they were antics until he went to his phone to see if she'd called or sent a message. There was none from her but there was one from his grandfather. The man said he'd gotten a call from an angry Felix Brandt about the "injustices" done to his daughter. Felix had admitted to sending Camille a copy of Remington's petition to run for mayor at his wife's request, saying that should prevent Remington from embarrassing his daughter any further. Remington fumed because he'd thought he and Felix were friends. He wanted to confront the instigating man, but felt it was more important to find Camille first and explain his actions before she fled and disappeared from his life forever.

He weighed his options, knowing that he could probably get dressed quickly and hop into his car and catch

Camille, but he eventually decided against that. He needed to be smart and figure out a way they could have it all. He needed to come up with a plan where he could have his wife *and* his life. There would be no convincing Camille if he didn't come prepared with a defense and proof they could be together without her career interfering. And though he didn't know if that were true, he'd definitely try to make it happen for them.

Remington needed a lawyer before he got too deep into this. He needed someone who would be willing to dig into the morality clause of his company and give him an honest, objective answer to the question of how the company could deal with the fallout from her announcement, if there was any. He also needed to prove to Camille that she wouldn't jeopardize his run for mayor. It was indeed a seemingly impossible task, being that they lived in Fairdell, but he had confidence in himself and the people who loved Camille to make this happen for her. And after a few calls and some explaining, he had his allies in place. But first there was a person he needed to see. He got into his car.

Sonya had set this course of events into motion by crying to her mother and father. She'd have to be set straight so she wouldn't cause any further problems for him and Camille. He just hoped the woman wouldn't do anything unreasonable or out of line during his visit. He didn't want to have to hurt her feelings since he wasn't that type of man, but he would if she continued to threaten the future he was trying to build with the woman he loved.

He wondered what had provoked Sonya to go to her

father, but if Remi really thought about it, it was obvious that she was jealous of Camille. She'd no doubt thought Remington would eventually give up on running from her and give in to his grandfather's original wishes. She had not anticipated the old man's easy acceptance of Camille and her career. She must've decided to go to the one person who could deny her nothing—her father. Felix Brandt had been the one to advise Remi on his run for office. The man had known about the petition and had been the one to call him when it had been approved. Needless to say, Sonya's mother had seen this as a step toward her daughter, never thinking Remington might have other plans for his personal life. It was probably a personal insult to both of her parents for Remington to dismiss their daughter even though he had never agreed to any type of future with Sonya.

Remi was suffering from a case of complete frustration. He clutched his hands tightly on the steering wheel of his car as he thought about what he could lose. Not the election or the company he ran, but Camille. Losing her again wasn't an option.

On the way he talked to her father and asked him to try to keep her in Fairdell. He texted Anna about moving up Camille's coming-out party. Then he talked to Charlie and asked him to look over the ethics and morality clauses in the company contract and the man had given him better news than he expected—news about Camille that could help sway the town's opinion. She'd been donating anonymously to the town's recreation center. Her generous contributions had kept the place open and the kids off the street. Only Charlie knew of her donations because he was her lawyer. The information was more than Remi could've hoped for—ammunition if it came to that.

Then Remi called his grandfather, and Frederick did not hesitate to extend his support, saying once he was done, the majority of the town would see Camille as a saint. Remi was grateful for everyone's help, especially from Camille's father and Charlie. Those two men could've left him to deal with it all by himself after the way his omission was hurting Camille, but they did not. Both had said they wouldn't allow her to sacrifice her happiness again no matter what Camille said.

It was time people started making sacrifices for her and not the other way around.

It was late in the evening, but Remington couldn't wait to complete this errand. He knew it could wait until the next day, but he wouldn't be able to sleep knowing this issue was hanging over him. He needed Sonya to call her father off and tell the man the truth. He'd done some thinking on the way over and the only conclusion he could come to was that Sonya had lied about the nature of their relationship to her mother and father. He'd make sure she set her parents straight before her father started a slander campaign against Camille. Remington could deal with the man coming after him, but Camille was off-limits.

"I'm going to go by and be with Camille," Remington recalled Charlie saying as he took another street that would lead him to his destination. Remi couldn't believe the possessive, involuntary growl that had erupted from deep within him at Charlie's words. Remi had known there wasn't anything romantic in the suggestion, but he couldn't help his reaction. Though, Charlie didn't seem at all bothered and had actually chuckled. "I'm going to try and calm her, so she won't bolt. She'll listen—I think. I'm sure she was more shocked by the news. But you do realize that it won't get past her that you knew about this long before she returned. She'll not let that go very easily."

It had made him angry with himself for keeping anything from Camille. He didn't regret his decision but he didn't like that he'd hurt Camille with his omission. He'd do it all over again the same way if it meant Camille was closer to being his than not, but the guilt was still there.

But if he lost her...

No. He couldn't lose her. It was not an option.

Chapter 19

"Remington? What brings you by so late? Is something wrong?"

Sonya smirked as she reached for her robe. Remi thought she was trying to close it more, but she instead uncovered just a bit more cleavage, allowing her hand to linger to garner his attention.

"We need to talk."

Pushing past Sonya, he walked into the living room of her home. She lived alone in a house her father had purchased for her. It was a nice house; he'd been in it on several occasions when their families had traded places for events they shared. He remembered having a good time in the space, but now being there made him uncomfortable and angry.

"I'm sorry, Remi," Sonya blurted, but it sounded

more like an invitation for something else rather than an apology. She closed the distance between them and placed a hand on his chest. "I'm really sorry for what Daddy has done, but—"

Remington looked down at the inappropriately placed hand. He then looked back to her. Not wanting to react too hastily while alone in her home, he gently removed her hand. "There is no 'but,' Sonya. I am with Camille and you need to accept that or—"

"Or what?" Sonya fumed. "Us being together was always the plan, Rem. It's what my parents want and what your parents would've wanted, God rest their souls."

"Don't call me that and don't you bring my parents into this. Don't try to guilt me into being with you. It won't work." Remington rubbed a hand down his face and put distance between them. "I thought I could come over here and talk reasonably with you—let you know how I felt without hurting your feelings, but—"

Remington's words stopped when Sonya dramatically collapsed to the floor in tears. "Do you hate me so much that I can't even call you by the nickname she gave you? I love you, Remi," she said once her act had ceased.

Remington rolled his eyes and asked God for help in this. He took a deep breath and sighed. "Sonya… you and I both know that you don't love me. You love the idea of who I am or what I may become, but you don't love me. Can we at least be honest here?" Remi asked, frustrated with Sonya's dramatics. When she didn't answer he leaned back on one of the barstools in her family room and continued. "We have never had a relationship and you know that. I don't know what you told your father, but you need to fix this. I am engaged. There is nothing temporary about Camille and me. I need you to accept that."

"I can't accept what I feel isn't right. She's not right for you, Remi. I am. I can be—"

"A friend. And if you aren't willing to be that then I suggest we cut all ties to one another. As a matter of fact, I think it would be best if you started searching for another place to work. I'm giving you ninety days to do so. I'll help in any way I can, but I doubt it'll be in the way you want. I can't be what you want, Sonya. It doesn't matter what your feelings are about my fiancée because it won't change the way I feel about her."

Remington's anger was ratcheting up so he decided he needed to calm down and take a different approach. "You once told me you wanted to be happy. If that wasn't a lie then you should realize a marriage of convenience and circumstance is not what you want," Remington said sincerely, hoping that taking a softer approach would get through to her.

Moving to help Sonya from the floor, Remington reached for her but she refused his offer. She stood on her own, closing her robe that had fallen open. Sonya then looked to him and he knew all the fight had left her when her eyes met his. "You're right, Remi. I did tell you that. But…but I also have a mother who expects me to—"

Remi knew it was a risk, but he placed his hands on her arms and she immediately stopped talking. She was hopeful for a moment and then deflated as he spoke.

"Your father is a good man and I'm sure all he wants is for you to be happy, your mother, as well. You'll find the man who's meant for you and, hey…if he's rich and good-looking all the better, right?"

Nodding and smiling slightly, Sonya said, "Remington Krane, you are truly a wonderful man with a big heart and… I'm sorry. This town will be lucky to have you as their mayor and I'll make sure my father doesn't do anything to make the journey harder."

Remi stepped away from Sonya. He turned away from her. There was nothing left to say. He believed her words and had known her long enough to see through her tricks. This was no trick.

"But don't think I'll be singing Camille's praises anytime soon," she added. "I may want you to be happy, but I couldn't care less about your precious 'Love Bug.'"

"Ladybug," he corrected, looking back over his shoulder. "And thank you for being honest. I never expected you to want to fake a friendship with her. I just ask that you back off and respect my happiness."

"I can do that. For you." Remington raised an eyebrow in question, hoping he hadn't been wrong about her previous sincerity. "Friends, remember? Oh, and I'll expect a hefty compensation package and glowing references."

Remington chuckled. He felt as if a weight had been lifted from his shoulders. However, there was still the issue of whether or not he and Camille were still a couple. Because if they weren't, this was all for nothing. He wished he could go and see her, talk to her. He wished he could explain, but Camille would need more than just

his words for her to believe they could make it through
the scrutiny and still have the life they'd dreamed about
as teenagers. She'd need tangible evidence and he'd
make sure she had that. She'd need to see the truth with
her own eyes. Because now that she'd returned to him
and introduced him to such passion and love, Remington wasn't about to give that up without a fight.

Camille had shown up at home and had gone to be
alone to look over the documents that had been sent
to her home. At first she wondered who could've done
this to them, but then she realized it didn't matter. The
information in those documents was the truth and who
exposed Remi wasn't important.

The date on the initial petition was months ago,
which meant Remington had been keeping his secret
the whole time. He could've volunteered the information, but he'd chosen to keep it to himself. And while
she believed in her heart he'd done it with good intent,
it didn't change the facts. She was still a writer of erotic
fiction and the people of Fairdell wouldn't see him as
a kind, God-fearing, capable leader if she was his potential first lady. She'd been willing to deal with being
the wife of the president of Krane Foods. Krane was a
business and as Frederick had said, no one could deny
she'd done well for herself on the business end. Her
writing could've been explained away as a career, one
she'd chosen before she and Remi fell in love. But with
politics, things weren't always so black and white. There
was a gray area that made someone with a career like
hers an easy target for people in a town like theirs. It

would boil down to the immorality of her career and Remington would lose because the devout would no longer trust or believe in his ability. They'd think Camille could influence him—his faith—because of the words in her books. It was a disaster waiting to happen.

Camille had fallen asleep with the copy of the petition lying next to her.

She woke to a knock on her door some time before midnight. Charlie. He demanded to talk to her. She'd refused...until he said, "I think you may be able to marry Remi."

Camille figured that Anna and her father had filled Charlie in on what was going on. But if that was the case then how did he think he already had a solution? It made Camille curious. Was it really possible Charlie had found a solution to her problems?

She let Charlie pull her from her room and down the steps, past the living room where a sleeping Anna lay on the love seat and on into the attached dining room. Once they sat at the table he asked her to tell her version of the events since she'd arrived in town. She wondered why he was bothering, but she told him everything—from when she arrived up until she woke up to his insistent knocking on her bedroom door. And she didn't just recall the events, she made sure Charlie understood her feelings of joy and happiness as well as the pain she felt when she realized she'd have to leave Remington because she knew he would never be the one to admit he needed to let her go.

"Why are you asking me to tell you all of this? It's taken over an hour and saying it aloud has done noth-

ing but make me surer of my decision. I have to go back
to New York and forget about Remington Krane…for
good this time. I can't ever come back here," Camille
said, resigned to her fate.

"And what about Reese?"

"I can fly him out to see me or we can take vacations
together or—" Charlie gave her a look. It was obvious
he knew Reese Ryan just as well as she did. The man
would never put up with her flying him all over the
place to see her, never returning to her family home.
"What are you getting at and what is it that you had to
tell me earlier? You said—"

"I lied." Camille gaped at Charlie. He shrugged. "I
had to get you to open the door. But it was also proof
and an admission that you aren't ready to give up on
being Mrs. Krane just yet."

Anna giggled from her perch on the love seat. Apparently she hadn't been asleep and had heard the conversation. She sat up with her hair falling behind her
and said, "He's right and you know it."

"He may be right but Charlie lied about being able
to help, Anna. There's no way to change the facts. And
what kind of wife would I be to Remi anyway? I can't
remember the last time I went to church. And can you
imagine me trying to host a dinner party or plan some
charity event? I am what you'd call persona non grata
in this town, nor am I very social. Certainly not the
wife of a mayor."

Anna shook her head. "This is just you trying to
come up with excuses—"

"Facts, not excuses," Camille huffed. "I'm done talking about this." Rising from her seat at the small table and nearly knocking her chair over, Camille ambled over to the sectional couch and propped her foot up on the ottoman. Looking at the piece of furniture made her insides clench in longing and remembrance. She and Remi had been intimate on this spot. Despite Camille's heartache, the memory made her smile.

"How about you don't make any decisions tonight, maybe wait a few days?" Charlie said and plopped down next to Camille. He brought her out of her pleasant reverie and then pulled her petite form to his side. "We'll have clear heads in the morning. We can talk about it then, right, Anna?"

Anna grunted and then turned into one of the couch pillows. She was so strange sometimes. Camille had never seen the woman sleep in a bed. She even slept on the couch in her own home. Camille shook her head and yawned. She ignored Charlie's declaration and said, "I'm going to fly out in the next day or so. I'm sure Anna and I will have to come up with a new plan of action for my big reveal. You and Daddy should come to New York for a few days."

"Not to burst your bubble, but the publisher thinks having the reveal here in your hometown is more personal and I'm inclined to agree," Anna said as if she wasn't asleep a few moments ago.

"Surely we can get that changed."

Anna hesitated, but stood by her initial response. Camille suspected there was more Anna wasn't telling her, but decided she needed to listen to Charlie and get some rest. It was already three in the morning.

* * *

A few days had passed and Remington was on edge. He'd yet to hear from Camille, but he knew she was still in town. He'd reached out to Reese and the man had told him that he needed to hurry and do whatever it was he was going to do because Anna had flown out to deal with another client and it was getting harder to convince Camille to stay until her event was held.

He'd had that conversation the day before and now he stood before Reese after a very interesting church service.

"Your grandfather is something else," Reese said to Remi. He couldn't help but agree. Frederick had decided that he needed to give a twenty-minute testimony and had spoken of his deteriorating health and had worked up to a near sermon over the importance of not judging others unless the person doing the judging was willing to succumb to the same scrutiny. He'd talked of love of family and community and how life was too short to allow petty biases to rule thoughts and opinions. He'd also spoken about losing Remington's father in that accident at sea, which he rarely did in front of others. He'd ended with announcing Remington's engagement to Camille as well as proclaiming that Remington would be the town's next mayor. By the time he was done, those in the church were shouting and agreeing with Frederick Krane's every word.

Remi had not known if the reaction had been genuine, but applause had erupted and nearly every member of the congregation had come to congratulate the three men—Reese, Frederick and Remington. Some had even volunteered to help with his campaign. It had been an overwhelming display of support and proof that he and Camille would be fine. He only wished she could've been there to see it for herself. It might have convinced her.

Yes, his grandfather certainly was something else. He shook his head. "Yes, he's full of surprises."

Remington and Reese talked for a few more minutes— mostly about Camille. Her father said she still wore the ring he gave her, which was a good sign. The bad sign? She'd locked herself up with her laptop and was only coming out of her room to eat or drink. She was avoiding him and Charlie now that Anna had left. She gave mostly one-word answers and tried to blame her reclusive mood on her writing. Remi knew better and so did her father.

As they left the early morning service, Remington couldn't take his mind off Camille and her need to protect him. Even as he ate lunch that afternoon with his grandfather, he couldn't stop thinking about his conversation with Reese. Remington wondered if this was her usual way to write or if their situation had driven her into hiding. He had a feeling this was all his fault. He'd handled the situation very poorly and this was the result.

His guilt had mounted substantially because of what Reese had described to him. And not because of what she was going through now, not completely. It was because he imagined her dealing with this kind of decision as an eighteen-year-old girl. He couldn't fathom being so selfless at that age. He wouldn't have been able to think so far ahead into the future, putting their goals and dreams ahead of what he wanted at the time.

Remi didn't realize he was doing it, but he'd risen from the table. His grandfather gave him a strange look. He dismissed the man and mumbled an apology. This separation was done. He could no longer wait for Charlie to review the company's codes and bylaws. He no longer cared about being mayor. If the people of Fairdell were going to be hypocrites and judge Camille when she had not committed a sin against any of them, then maybe they weren't the people he really wanted to lead.

"I expect you to have my future granddaughter-in-law with you for the next Sunday lunch," the old man shouted at Remington as he disappeared through the dining room. Remington hoped that he would.

Camille was still crying through her smile as she sat on her bed. If she hadn't seen it for herself, she would have never believed it, but thanks to her father, she'd just witnessed something amazing.

She received a text from her father with a link attached and she wondered why he was texting during church service. She'd opened the link he'd sent and when the window opened it took Camille a little while to realize she was watching the service on the church's website. She wasn't sure if it was live or a recording, but it didn't matter because it wouldn't change the content.

That morning her father had insisted she attend with him, but she wouldn't. Remi attended the same church and she couldn't see him. She'd definitely not be able to resist him and she'd give in to the promises she knew he couldn't keep—promises of realizing the dream they'd had as teenagers. So she'd declined the invitation for that reason, as well as not wanting to deal with the scathing glances of the other parishioners.

Now, as she watched on her laptop, she saw Remington's grandfather, Frederick Krane, standing before the church speaking passionately. She gasped as she listened to the man pour his heart out as he declared his support of his grandson's engagement to Camille and his run for mayor.

She was now crying because she was moved by the elder Krane's words and overwhelmed by the response of the congregation.

Camille wasn't sure if this had happened at the first or second service, but in that moment she decided she was done sacrificing. If the people in the town couldn't put aside their biases after a speech like that, then maybe Remi should reconsider wanting the job of leading such a judgmental gathering of souls.

She could admit to herself it was why she had yet to leave Fairdell. She still had hope. Camille just needed the right motivation. How ironic it was that it came from a man who'd once disapproved of her entire existence in Remi's life.

There wasn't a time Camille could remember showering and getting ready so quickly. But she groaned at her appearance in the mirror, skeptical about the dress she had to wear. She'd brought three dresses to choose from for her dinner with the distributor and the one she had on now was the last of them. It was a black dress in a conservative silhouette, but that's where the innocence ended. Her legs were on display halfway up her thigh and the fabric fit snugly to her curvy form. There were tasteful mesh accents that didn't reveal much, but it was definitely not appropriate for church.

Stepping into her heels before she lost her nerve, Camille rushed from her room and down the steps. When she got to the garage and saw that the only vehicle left was her father's truck, she cursed and then asked forgiveness for using the word on a Sunday.

Looking down at her gold watch, Camille swore again. She didn't remember what time church ended but it was after one in the afternoon and she was probably cutting it close to the end of the second service. If the video was a recording from the first service, she was already too late. Once again she let an expletive fall from her lips in frustration.

"Cursing on a Sunday, Ladybug. What would your father think?"

She cursed again and whirled around to face the most wonderful sight. Remi stood there looking quite confident in a light gray suit and a crisp white button-down with no tie. The first couple of buttons on his shirt were undone, revealing a glimpse of the smooth caramel skin she'd enjoyed touching and kissing. Looking up into his eyes she saw what she'd seen reflected in her own eyes in the mirror, only moments ago.

They were both done sacrificing their happiness for the sake of others.

The most beautiful sight greeted Remi when he emerged from his car. He didn't know how she didn't hear the car, but she looked panicked and rushed and oh so damn sexy. He had no idea where she was headed in that getup, but he hoped he could be invited for the ride. Shaking his head, he realized where his thoughts had gone and refocused his attention on Camille and her complete surprise over seeing him and her appreciative assessment of his form as he stood before her.

"Remi? What are you doing here? I..." Next thing he knew, he was being attacked. Camille attached herself to him, baby chimp style, leaving parts of her exposed that shouldn't be exposed. "I'm so sorry, Remi. I was so wrong. I know what your grandfather said and I saw... I don't care about everyone else. I just want to be with you." And with that admission, she was kissing him all over his face, telling him they'd find a way to work it out.

Then suddenly she was gone. She slid down his body, suddenly embarrassed by her actions. He wasn't complaining; he was just stunned. He'd come here to say something along those lines, and that, mixed with the way she'd thrown her body at him, had Remington trying to process what had just happened.

Had she just said she'd heard what his grandfather had said at church? How could that be?

Putting the pieces together, Remington stepped back. She must've seen the live stream or the recording of the service and had thought it to be the proof of support she needed, just as he had. Then he stifled a chuckle.

"You were going to wear *that* to church?" While the dress looked great, it wasn't church clothes.

"Shut up! I'm out of clean clothes."

Not wanting her to think he didn't like her attire, he stepped back into Camille's personal space. Her skin enticed him with its smell and her body enticed him with its closeness.

Damn. What had he come over here for?

It no longer mattered because they were once again on the same page and she wanted him no matter what they'd have to deal with from those around them. That thought completely fled his mind when she turned around and walked away. The globes of her rear shifted and bounced taking turns as if the movement was meant to hypnotize him into following. It worked. He followed her, all the way to her room. The sound of her lock engaging snapped him out of his haze, but not before Camille's hand reached for the part of him that desired her touch the most. He was a goner and couldn't think of why he'd wanted to stop.

Camille surprised Remi by going onto her knees and giving him more pleasure than he'd ever felt from any woman. The way she caught on to his silent instruction heightened the gratification behind this act. He had to stop her before—

He should feel embarrassed but he didn't. Camille was so intuitive and so good at what she was doing that she didn't allow him to be embarrassed for coming after only a couple minutes of being treated to her inexperienced, yet skilled mouth. She lapped at him as he came down, not wasting a drop, which had him hard all over again before he'd come down from his first release.

"I didn't come here for that," Remi declared and the sound of his own voice was strange to his ears. It sounded as if he'd been holding his breath for much too long.

"I know."

Camille's phone was going off and Remington encouraged her to answer while he caught his breath and got himself together. She giggled with a little arrogance at his reaction to her efforts.

She said it was Anna calling from downstairs. The agent had returned so they could move forward with the party plans. What Camille didn't know was that he'd never stopped planning their engagement party along with her friends. He'd already accepted the fact that Charlie may not have good news for him and was already trying to think of a contingency plan if that were the case.

"Are you ready for what we're about to face, Ladybug?"

"No."

Remington pulled the phone from his future wife's hand and guided her into the warm circle of his embrace. He understood her hesitation, but they were in this together and he made sure he told her that with his words as well as a passionate kiss.

"I think I'll change first." She looked down at herself. "I have no idea what I was thinking. I'm glad you saved me from embarrassing myself."

"I love you, Ladybug."

"I love you, too, Rem."

Remington sighed at the endearment and left Camille's room before he wasn't able to do so.

From the moment she'd turned and seen Remi standing in front of her house, Camille had known what they had to face and had just wanted one moment of normalcy before their lives exploded. She didn't know why she chose *that* particular form of normalcy, but the overwhelming urge had come over her in the moment and she'd gone with it, and when it was over, she felt alive and in control. An animalistic sensation had coursed through her at the way she'd claimed Remington and the manner in which he'd responded. It was that adrenaline rush and boost of confidence that was pushing her to move forward with revealing herself as Reese Elaine. Maybe once this event was done, then she and Remi could think about how to handle their engagement party.

When she arrived in the family room, Anna, Charlie, Remington and her father were there. They were in the midst of discussing something but they all immediately fell silent when she appeared at the threshold.

Remi gestured for her to come over and join him on the couch and she did. She was still really tired after her four-day-long writing marathon and subsequent crying session from the night before, not that she'd admit the latter to anyone. She'd been writing and when she'd taken a break she'd been trying to figure out a way she and Remi could make their relationship work. Every time each solution she came up with seemed as if it would end in disaster, she'd cry and accept her fate once again.

Kissing the finger where her engagement ring rested, Remington then helped Camille get comfortable and cuddle into his side. She was thankful for his warmth even though her needing him next to her had nothing to do with the temperature. She didn't want to be apart from him again anytime soon. Those days had been agony.

Chapter 20

Camille was curled up at his side like a little kitten looking for attention. It was so uncharacteristic of her to be this way—this vulnerable—and he knew he had to hurry and get them through the impending chaos. He could see how easy it was for her to shut off the world and become withdrawn and reclusive as her father had said she'd done. It was obvious that it was a defense mechanism for his gorgeous little Ladybug and he didn't want her to ever have to hide again. He wanted her to be the confident woman who'd controlled his pleasure only moments ago in her bedroom. He never wanted her to get used to hiding her identity again or feeling as if she should be ashamed of what she'd chosen to do for a living.

And it wasn't that he didn't enjoy the way she was

attached to him. He did. Immensely. He especially liked the way her hand had crept under the hem of his dress shirt and had settled against the bare skin of his stomach. It was as if she needed that skin-to-skin connection to him and he wouldn't deny her that.

In the last few days Camille had worked through a lot. She'd talked to her father about her issues with forgiving herself for her mom's death. She'd decided she needed a clean slate in her life if she and Remi were to move forward. Forgiving and forgetting was on the top of both of their lists. Remi had been able to forgive her for what she'd done ten years ago and she'd been able to forgive him for his recent omission. What did they have to be angry about, really? They'd both attempted to do the right thing by protecting the person they loved. And while their actions had left some hurt feelings in their wake, it had been for the best of reasons— for each other.

It had been an enlightening few days that turned into two weeks of craziness and frustration. Camille had been called back to New York and gone through a whirlwind of business meetings and appointments to get her moved as soon as possible. Anna had even roped her into shopping for a new dress for her party in Fairdell, which had kept her away from Remi that much longer. They'd talked on the phone every day and texted nonstop and now it was time to return to her man and the life she'd chosen.

Camille couldn't wait.

But obviously someone thought she could, because as

she sat on the plane to fly her back to Fairdell, the pilot had the nerve to come over the intercom and announce they had to return to the gate and wait out the inclement weather. That delay only lasted for about two hours, and now, safe and sound, they were landing in Georgia. She was about to face the biggest night of her life.

"You ready for this, Ladybug? I mean we could just back out now. We could have the driver turn the car around and I could take you back home and peel every last stitch of this sexy white dress off you. Then I could show you that thing you like…you know the thing I do with my—"

Camille turned to look at her handsome fiancé with his freshly shaven head and his low beard that she loved. He was serious. If she said the word, he'd take her away and ravage her. She wanted that more than anything right now. Especially being that he'd been flirting for the whole ride from the airport to his home, where she'd changed, and on over to the local Performing Arts Theater where her party was being held.

"We can't, Rem," Camille cut him off, but it had no conviction behind it. There was nothing but lust and desire in her words, as if she dared him to make his words come true.

"Maybe not, but this is your party and you can arrive when you please." He then told the limo driver to take a half-hour detour. Camille stared at Remi with bated breath as he spoke, knowing what was about to happen.

Before Camille could conjure another thought, Remi was all over her. His lips crashed to hers and instinct took over. Her hands flew to the sides of his face, accepting his tongue as it rolled and lapped and caressed the corners and crevices of her mouth. Camille moaned and wiggled in her tight dress, feeling like the thin fabric was much too confining. Remi's hand had found its way around her waist and settled on the small of her back and was pulling her closer with each deep moan that escaped her lips.

She was aware that they should not be doing this but she was unable to deny herself. This man was her addiction and she still was unsure how she'd managed to stay away from him for ten long years. She constantly needed his hands on her as she was utterly obsessed with the feel of his touch.

Even now as his hands roamed her back, looking for the zipper of her dress, Camille still did not feel as if it was enough.

Once she was dressed only in her red pumps—a color that matched the hue of the lipstick that was now all over Remi's face—he stopped her. "Leave them on," he growled.

Remi quickly undressed and pulled Camille onto his lap, skillfully impaling her. After that, there was nowhere he did not touch or caress or kiss as they made love like hormonal teenagers after prom, determined to lose their virginity.

Any night with Camille was one Remington looked forward to, but this night was truly incredible. He reveled in her surprise when they finally reached the theater and she saw that nearly everyone in the town had come. He and Anna had worked closely to arrange the event that not only celebrated the town's famous citizen, but also their engagement, and the kickoff of Remington's mayoral campaign. Camille had been beyond ecstatic, knowing the party had turned into such an affair, and laughed with glee.

He'd have to work on her and help her come out of her shell if she was going to be his first lady, but Remi had the utmost confidence that Camille would eventually come around.

David had been a little jealous he wasn't more involved in the party planning, but understood the circumstances once Remi had confided in his friend.

The press was going crazy, having the real name of the elusive author who'd been able to fool them for so long. Two different producers had already approached Camille with requests for meetings about turning her books into movie scripts. She'd graciously deferred them to Anna who was on cloud nine with the new fame she'd garnered as Reese Elaine's agent.

Another pleasant surprise for Remi was the reaction of the town. They embraced Camille with open arms. Camille reveled in the drama-free night and he rejoiced in her happiness.

It wasn't just Camille's happiness Remington celebrated. He had his own joy to be thankful for. He'd not known how incomplete his life had been in Camille's absence. He had not known the meaning of true satisfaction and contentment until Camille had returned to him.

Would they have issues to work through because of their different choices and different paths in life thus far? Yes. They'd have plenty to overcome in that regard, but they had each other and that was more than they'd ever anticipated for themselves not long ago.

"Is tonight everything you imagined it would be?" Remington asked Camille as he led her across the floor when the final song of the evening started playing just for them. Remi couldn't be prouder of this beautiful woman before him, who held his heart. She made him want to do anything and everything to make sure a smile stayed etched into her features.

Beaming with delight, Camille responded. "Better than I imagined." She sighed contentedly and Remi was happy he was part of the reason she was able to feel so good. "Who'd have thought we'd ever be here in this moment?"

"Haven't you heard?" Remington asked, unable to restrain himself from kissing Camille when she wore such a contented smile. "I never gave up on you. Your return to me was always the plan, it just took you a lot longer to realize you couldn't stay away."

Camille's eyes watered and she shook her head as a little chuckle fell from her lips. She then laid her head on his chest and he could tell she was trying to hold back her emotions. Lifting her chin, he stared into her glossy eyes for a brief moment and then kissed her again. He didn't need her to confirm or deny his statement. Her reaction was enough.

Epilogue

Camille couldn't believe that a simple visit to care for her father had turned into such a life-changing return to her hometown. She still thought about that time over a year and half ago when she'd finally decided to stop sacrificing her happiness and stop running. She remembered choosing, after much agonizing, to be a little selfish and take everything she wanted, consequences be damned.

And now look what she had to show for her courage. She was blessed and loved more than she ever could have expected being Mrs. Camille Krane.

Though, in addition to her new status as a wife, she was able to successfully come out from under her pseudonym and put a face to the name many readers loved so much. The success she'd attained after her coming-out party had been overwhelming, humbling and more than she could have ever fathomed.

Never did Camille think she would be able to have such success and happiness while getting everything she'd dreamed of having since she was a teenager. The reality was she had that and so much more.

Camille smiled because it was always satisfying when she thought about the decision she'd made as a teen to marry Remington. Over a decade later they'd finally fulfilled the promise they'd made to be together and she couldn't be happier with her personal *and* professional life.

Her husband wasn't doing so bad for himself, either. With the land deal he'd successfully negotiated over a year ago, Krane Gourmet Snack Foods was no longer second best. They'd surpassed their competitors with the opening of the new frozen foods division and were currently weighing the benefits of overseas headquarters and expansion.

It was just too bad her husband wasn't going to be working on that firsthand. Remington worked as an integral part of the decision-making, but his day-to-day duties with Krane Foods were minimal. He'd put the company's daily operations into the capable hands of his vice president.

Camille liked to think that these days her husband had much more important matters to handle, like overseeing the city that had become just as prosperous as the company he'd previously led.

"Have everything you need?" Remington asked after

placing a heaping bowl of vanilla ice cream in Camille's hand and proceeding to rub her tired, swollen feet.

Camille nodded. She had everything she needed and wanted, but she still giggled each time she took in her surroundings. A year and a half after nearly walking away from Remington again, Camille was sitting on her large bed at the mayor's estate, rubbing a large belly filled with her twin son and daughter. She smiled at the changes and said a silent prayer of thanks to God for showing her the right path and opening her eyes to what and who she needed in her life.

The gorgeous man before her, who was mayor of their loving little town, smiled as well, as if he knew her thoughts. The look quickly morphed into something more and...

The ice cream could wait.

* * * * *

REQUEST YOUR FREE BOOKS!

2 FREE NOVELS PLUS 2 *FREE GIFTS!*

KIMANI™
ROMANCE

Love's ultimate destination!

*Four years ago Kara Goshay believed a vicious lie
about Virgil Bougard and ended their relationship.
And even after her apology, Virgil is still bitter.
Now his family firm has hired Kara's PR company to
revamp his playboy image. But faking a liaison with
Kara for the media backfires when the line between
fantasy and reality is blurred by strong sexual
attraction. The stakes are high—but so is their searing
desire, a connection so intense it could possibly tame
this elusive, unforgiving bachelor at last...*

*Read on for a sneak peek at
BACHELOR UNFORGIVING, the next exciting
installment in* New York Times *bestselling author
Brenda Jackson's* **BACHELORS IN DEMAND** *series!*

His eyes were so cold she felt the icy chill all the way to
her bones. She took a deep breath and then said, "Hello,
Virgil."

He didn't return her greeting, just continued to give
her a cold stare. But she pushed on. "May I speak with
you privately for a minute?"

"No. We have nothing to say to each other."

Virgil's tone was so hard Kara was tempted to turn
and walk away. But she refused to do that. She would

get him alone even if she had to provoke him into it. She lifted her chin, met his gaze and smiled ruefully. "I understand you not wanting to risk being alone with me, Virgil. Especially since you've never been able to control yourself where I'm concerned."

The narrowing of Virgil's eyes indicated she might have gone too far by bringing up their past relationship and reminding him of how taken he'd once been with her.

He continued to stare at her for the longest time. Silence surrounded the group, and she figured Virgil was well aware the two of them had not only drawn the attention of his godbrothers but a few others in the room who'd known they'd once been a hot item.

Finally Virgil slowly nodded. "You want to talk privately, Kara?" he asked in a clipped voice that was shrouded with a daring tone, one that warned she might regret the request. "Then, by all means, lead the way."

Don't miss BACHELOR UNFORGIVING
by Brenda Jackson, available August 2016
wherever Harlequin® Kimani Romance™
books and ebooks are sold!

KPEXP0716